Cara

Happily After When

A 12 book series, inspired by fairytales and the ugliness of real life.
Books are sequential, and highly recommended to be read in publication order.

J a z z
An Aladdin retelling

A r i a
A Little Mermaid Retelling

C a r a
A Cinderella Retelling

S a c h i
A Snow White Retelling

And more to follow...

HAPPILY AFTER WHEN BOOK 3

when power is stolen

Cara

EMILY BOURNE

First Published by Halo & Claws Publishing 2021

CARA

Happily After When - Book 3

Copyright © Emily Bourne 2021

For information contact: https://www.emilybourne.net

Stock Images via Bigstock, Shutterstock

ISBN: 978-1-925990-11-9 (Paperback)
ISBN: 978-1-925990-10-2 (Ebook)

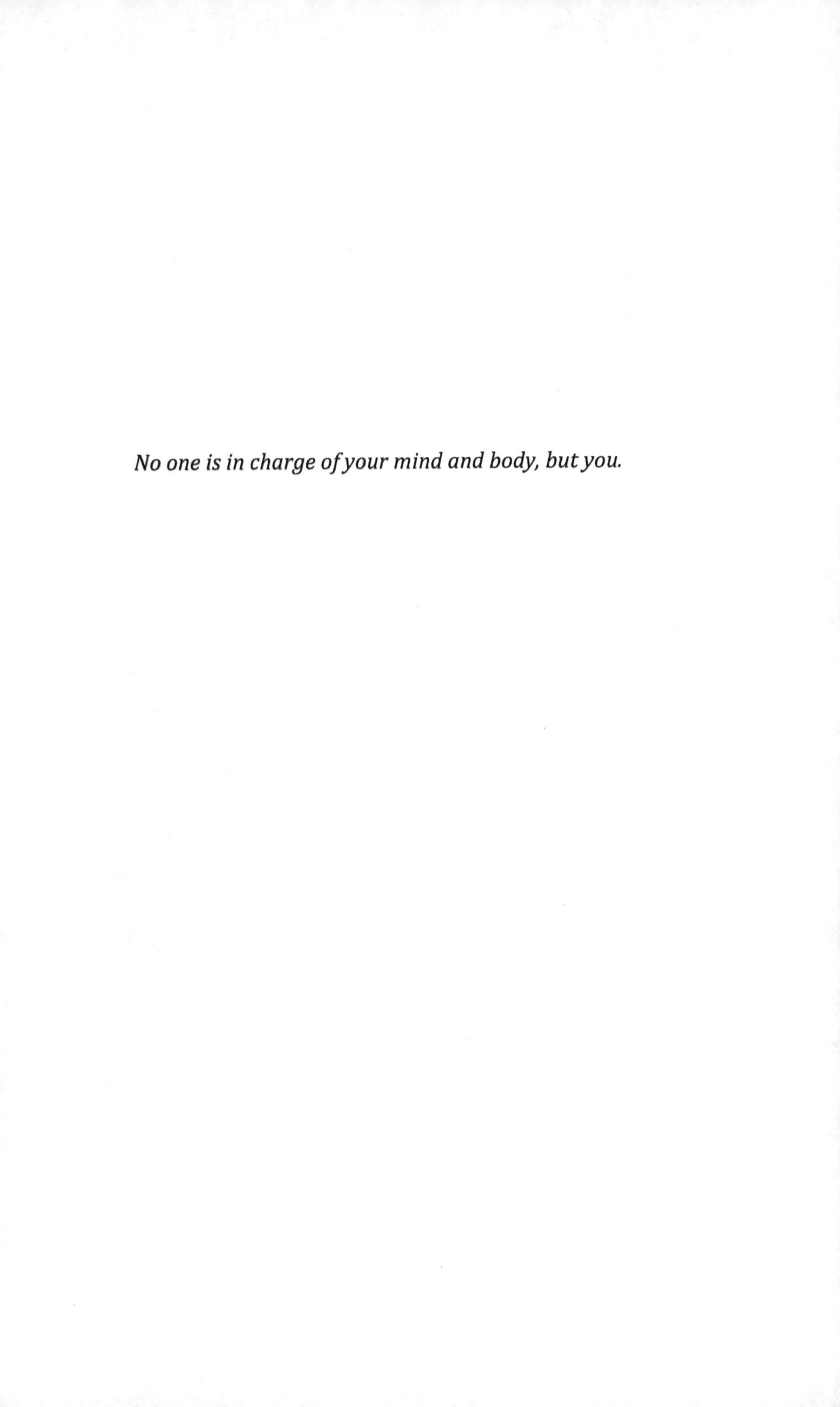

No one is in charge of your mind and body, but you.

Neon

Cara moves like there is a spotlight on her. Not wanting praise. Not wanting attention. More than anything, she does not want to be seen.

Always on guard, she makes decisions like every eye is watching her. This way there are no mistakes. This way no one will catch her.

The music from the DJ booth pulsates through the walls of the nightclub and jolts the floor. The neon lighting illuminates the patrons in purples and blues as they drink cocktails and grind on the dancefloor. Behind her dark tinted aviator sunglasses, Cara sees every individual perfectly. With years of training, she learnt to focus and rely on her peripheral vision. The added darkness is like a security blanket. Calmed by no one's ability to look directly into her eyes.

Cara scans the room and gauges the intoxication levels. Sometimes when her prey is too wasted, it is harder to complete the job. Their bodies flail unpredictably, and if she gets caught, they meet her with a mess of slurred and aggressive words. Something she rather not deal with.

Her eyes land on two preppy men, clinking pints of beer together. They lean against a cocktail table and throw their heads back with laughter. Cara's hands tingle with the urge to pick their pockets, as the men overtly leer at women, wanting a hook-up.

They deserve this.

She tilts her head as they provoke each other to approach another girl.

If I play the part of drunk girl, maybe they'll flash their cash on some food? It'd be good to eat something before moving on to other targets.

Cara sighs into a slump. She hates playing the drunk girl angle. It involves communicating with the creeps and letting them think they can have her. She twists her oily blonde hair over her shoulder, as she dips her dark shades slightly lower on the bridge of her nose. Her hips swing as she saunters over to them.

One guy nudges the other, a huge, cheesy grin taking up two-thirds of his face. Both men stare at Cara like a piece of meat.

Her stomach drops, but she ignores it as she scrutinises them. They wear light jackets, which will be easy to feel for anything of value in the pockets. Their tailored trousers have the signature two pockets at the front and none at the rear. The worst kind to sneak into.

Ick.

But they always let her. The fake drunk-girl-kinda-interested play is by far the easiest. It's like these guys are begging for her to do it.

"Hey there," one of them says. His dark blonde hair is slicked back and there is not a trace of stubble on his too clean face.

He's so shiny.

His friend is just as wax-looking, and pulls an arm around Cara to bring her close.

"Hey guys, what's up?" Cara says, so bubbly she can't stand it. She throws in a giggle and wants to punch herself.

Waxy guy's hand slides down her back, and Cara's insides shudder. She has learnt to mask her reactions on the outside, but is yet to master turning off inside. After years at this game, she'd hoped to deaden that part of her. Her gut will never let her. Always on guard. Trusting no one.

Cara slides a hand along his waist and taps the back of her hand against the inside of his jacket. *Mobile phone, wallet, loose cash. Easy, done.*

"Things are looking up now that you're here," Waxy says, smirking.

"What are you doing with these?" Shiny says, reaching for her glasses.

"Don't," she snaps.

They stare at her, dumbfounded.

She's quick to add a smile. "I love to add some mystery when meeting new people."

Shiny folds his arms and his smile slides left, intrigued. "Oh, mystery girl, ay. I like the sounds of that."

Cara traces a finger in a circle on Waxy's t-shirt. "You guys eating? I'm kinda down for some food."

"*Pfft.*" Waxy scoffs. "Food's no good. It doesn't let the drinks work fast enough."

"Hey, I'm down for more drinks too," Cara says, moving her arm from the inside of Waxy's coat, and leaning on Shiny. "I just want a burger too."

"Girls eating burgers is hot," Shiny says, enjoying Cara's body pressed against his.

Coins, gum packet... two mobile phones? Why does he need two?

"This place doesn't do burgers," Waxy says, somewhat agitated. Obviously pissed Cara's now leaning on his friend instead of him.

"Like *duh*," Cara says playfully. "There's the food truck out front. Let's eat, then you can buy me cocktails."

She giggles like she's had four martinis and slips her hand to Shiny's trouser pocket.

Shiny likes this a little too much for Cara's liking, and grabs her bum and squeezes hard.

Ouch, arsehole.

Her teeth grind, but she has perfected smiling over the top of it.

Shiny's face dips by hers, and he whispers with beer-stained breath, "Well, we can go outside, and ditch him in here."

"You'll get me that burger?" she whispers back.

"I'll give you all the meat you want."

Gross. He's wasting my time. I'll have to rob him because all he wants is me in an alley on my knees.

Not happening, Bucko.

Cara smiles at Shiny and slips back to Waxy. She leans into Waxy, and whispers, "And you're sure you don't wanna come?" as her hands pilfer his pockets.

His wallet slides out as her leg rubs against his. She flicks her wrist, and the wallet slides into the heavy-duty pocket of her bomber jacket. She takes the loose cash and phone. People notice the weight difference of a half-empty pocket, but not an empty one.

She works on the other pocket, leaning in closer so Shiny doesn't see her hands.

"Damn, girl, you seem like fun," Waxy says, grinning.

Cara giggles and pushes back to press against Waxy. Behind her, her hands dig in his pockets, unnoticed as the guys goofily laugh at each other.

"Will you fellas let me freshen up before we leave?"

"Do what you gotta do," Waxy says, salivating.

"I can't wait for the meat," Cara says, girlishly.

"Why wait?" Shiny whispers harshly in her ear, hands all over her bum. "We can head into the bathroom with you."

"It'll be worth the wait," Cara whispers back, sliding away.

He grabs her wrist and jerks her back.

Cara almost loses balance, but this isn't her first time in this dance. She turns her wrist over and twists his arm into a position where he's forced to let go. As soon as he does, she's quick to move. With her head down, she gets lost in the sea of purple and blue bodies that thump with the beat.

On her way, she unclips bracelets, flicks off watches, and picks pockets for loose cash.

She busts into the janitor's closet by the bar, scales the shelving, and swings herself up and through the broken window. For six months this window has been broken. For six months she has robbed the patrons. For six months, no one notices her re-offending.

The game is getting too easy.

Oof!

Cara's is slammed against the brick wall of the alley. Two tattooed men with neon-coloured hair hold her back. Cara pouts as

Dean approaches with a slow walk.

"Sup?" she says with a nod.

"I thought we had a deal, Girl," Dean says, dragging on a cigarette. "We are business associates, but then I find out, you're not holding up your end of the deal."

"What are you talking about?" Cara replies, playing it cool.

"For two weeks you haven't brought us clients," Dean says, blowing smoke in her direction. "How long did you intend to screw us around?"

"I'm not screwing you."

"*Dyke*," one of Dean's henchmen coughs.

Cara's eyes roll.

"I need buyers," Dean says, angling the ashy cigarette at Cara's cheek.

Cara swallows roughly. She's seen him do it before. A cigarette burn to the cheek would really make her memorable. She can't have any distinguishing marks in her line of work.

"How do you expect me to run a successful business and expand without more clients?" Dean says, angling his head so his strip of neon pink hair flaps against his shaved scalp.

"There are two guys inside," Cara says, calm and collected. "They're gonna be pissed because I took their stuff. One had two phones, so obviously living some double life. They look like they are Province kids. Probably at university. The three phones are in my pocket."

The henchman fishes inside her jacket pockets and pulls out phones, jewellery, and cash.

"The cash is mine," Cara snaps. "You can sell the phones or use them against the dudes to get them hooked."

"We're taking everything," Dean says, dragging his cigarette again. "Consider it payment for the last two weeks."

"I haven't worked for the past two weeks," Cara pleads. She had more pressing matters than finding people for The Neons to sell drugs to. "I need the cash."

Dean instructs the henchmen to let her go, and they move down the alley with her loot.

"Not my problem, sweetheart," Dean whispers with his gravelly, nicotine-damaged voice. "You wanna survive on these streets? You play by my rules."

He walks away with another puff of his cigarette and Cara wants to clock the back of his head. She balls up her fists and internalises the anger. A good rule of thumb is, don't deck the head of a street gang. It won't end well for you.

Shit. I really wanted that damn burger.

Distraction

Cara stretches her neck and shoulders, preparing to hit the next club.

She moves to the back of the alley but stops when her stomach growls.

Damn, I need to eat.

She had laid low in The Limits after a job turned south. It meant not eating for four or five days. She lost count after her stomach twisted in on itself. Then choosing to she shut off her mind to what she was depriving her body.

Cara pulls open a busted back door of a club that's always dark. Easy targets are a must. She's too hungry to play around. Underneath her jacket, she rubs her tender shoulder where Dean's guy restrained her. She knows better than to run from Dean. They don't need to make a big show for her to stop and listen to him.

But I guess they know how easily I could slip past them. They aren't as dumb as they look.

The club has minimal lighting, casting everyone in dark shadows. Even darker behind her glasses. No neon lighting, but the occasional strobe light. Cara uses the strobes to identify unguarded pockets, abandoned bags, and wasted clientele. The bar sounds like a perfect nightly target.

She wishes.

The patrons never hold much cash, making it hard to get a decent haul from this club alone. Kids from the top end of town are never here. Cara hates robbing these people. Desperate times call for desperate measures. Hopefully, someone is carrying drugs she can give to a Neon to sell. Even ten percent of the sale is a great payday for her.

Cara raids the pockets of two different couples in distracted embraces. She slides onto a stool and lays her head on the cocktail table. Her head throbs from a mixture of hunger and not being in the clubs for a week. She needs to get her head back in the game. The clubs are the only way she can survive living on the streets.

"Buy you a drink?" a voice offers beside her.

Cara angles her head to view the face the voice belongs to. It's near impossible to make out the figure between her dark glasses and the lack of light.

Cara could not care less and doesn't respond.

"You ok, love?" the voice comes through as female.

Cara has an urge to fall asleep.

"You need some water? Food?"

A lazy smile spreads on Cara's face.

"C'mon," the voice says, patting Cara's back. "I'm heading for a slice. Wanna join me?"

Cara rubs her head and turns to the shadowy face. "Burger?"

A hint of laughter plays against the loud music. "Sure. I can handle a burger."

The woman helps Cara up, but she's not into having someone else's hands on her, and busts ahead to the front doors.

"Hey, what's up?" the voice calls behind her when she reaches the midnight street.

Cara turns around and almost stumbles backwards as her shaded eyes land on one of the sexiest women she's ever seen. Her dark, curly hair is loosely pulled back. She wears a slim-fitting black t-shirt, a light jacket, and body-hugging leather pants.

There's just something about leather.

"What?" she says, looking Cara up and down.

"You still keen on a burger?" Cara asks, grinning.

Leather-girl nods as she moves closer, the streetlights dazzle her grey eyes.

"C'mon," she nods. "I know a good food truck."

"If it's the one by The Doghouse you do," Cara says, following.

"Really? The one on Bleaker Street is always good."

"Nah-uh. Bleaker Street is nothing compared."

"I'm Pippa," the girl in leather introduces herself.

Cara's steps hurry. Her go to strategy when avoiding her name.

"What made you come out tonight?" Pippa continues, two steps behind Cara.

"I'm always out," Cara replies quickly.

"I had an urge for vodka and darkness," Pippa says. "I didn't intend to come back out on the streets this soon."

Cara huffs, kicking her feet as she marches in an angry brisk pace.

"You can just go back inside then," Cara grumbles. "You're the one who suggested we get food."

"I wasn't going to let you pass out on the table."

Cara scoffs. "I wasn't gonna pass out. I was just taking a

minute to rest." Cara turns around to view Pippa eyeing her. She grumbles again and turns away. "Why don't you just leave me alone? I've got better things to do."

"You always wear dark glasses at night?" Pippa questions.

"What's it to you?"

"Just curiosity."

"Piss off."

"The Doghouse is at the end of the block," Pippa says. "I'm going. You can either have your bitch fit or come with me."

At this, Pippa's pace quickens, and she breaks past Cara, storming ahead.

Cara's pace drops, and she stands, watching the confidence in Pippa's stride. Her eyes land on the perky curve of her bum, and Cara's legs get moving again.

She meets Pippa at the food truck as she orders two burgers with the lot.

Thank Christ.

Pippa looks to Cara with a raised eyebrow. "Calmed down?"

Cara's eyes narrow. "Why do I have to be calm?"

"How else are you going to take in what's around you if you're not calm?"

"What, like the two hobos behind us playing tic-tac-toe? The girls turning tricks on the top corner, contemplating beating our arses so we don't steal their attention? Or the kid moving in the alley for a place to sleep or to buy drugs? I haven't worked out which he's after."

Pippa steps back, her mouth slightly ajar, as she takes Cara in.

"Don't tell me I'm not paying attention," Cara whispers harshly.

When their burgers are ready, they take one each and unwrap the paper. Cara takes a bite, and her insides light up with gratitude.

"*Oh yum,*" Pippa moans. "You're right," she says with a mouthful of burger. "So much freaking better."

Cara smiles while taking another bite.

She eats half the burger and then wraps up the rest and places it in her jacket pocket.

"How could you stop eating?" Pippa asks, salivating. "You couldn't pay me to stop."

Cara smirks. "I just eat in small bursts."

Pippa shrugs, lifting the burger to her lips. "Suit yourself."

"Well, thanks for the food," Cara says with a wave. "I've gotta head off."

Pippa eats the last of the burger and throws the wrapping in the trash while hurriedly wiping her mouth with the back of her hand.

"What do you mean?" Pippa says, catching up with her. "Where are you going?"

"I need to hit another club."

"Which one? I'm not ready to go home yet. Where should I go?"

"I'm not looking for someone to hang off me."

Pippa sniggers. "Like I'm going to cramp your style?"

Cara flicks her eyes at Pippa's body. *Her style would only be a distraction. I can't afford to be distracted.*

"C'mon. I'll buy you that drink now," Pippa suggests.

"I could do with a beer."

"Not a cocktail girl?"

"Do I look like a cocktail girl?"

"*Ha*, no. Are you going to tell me that name now?"

"I'll see how I feel after that drink," Cara says as she pushes open a door to a club that's heavy on the neon and warm bodies with loaded pockets.

Pippa moves towards the bar, and Cara taps her shoulder, shouting over the music that she's heading to the bathroom.

Cara moves to the rear of the club and scopes the talent in the room. The Province university crowd haven't disappointed. They are ripe for the picking.

She pushes through the line for the ladies' bathroom and girls squawk at her for cutting in, ready to pull hair or kick her with their stiletto heels.

Cara runs into one lavishly dressed Barbie doll who shrieks and spills her cosmopolitan.

"I'm so sorry," Cara says, helping the girl to stand while dipping her hand into the open purse. She slips the cash and pills into her pocket. Hoping it's something more than aspirin that she can trade for cash.

"Get away from me, you freak!" the Barbie yells.

Cara moves away from the line, swiping cash a guy left sitting by his drink as he chats up an intoxicated girl. She moves further into the club to the dancefloor. The easiest place to pick pockets because people are already eager to be felt up.

Cara slips between couples, searching for prime targets. A girl and guy grind against each other, and Cara notices a bulge in the guy's back pocket. He's so busy looking at her cleavage, he'll never notice.

She approaches the couple, but a hand pulls at her hip. Alarmed, she turns around and is met by the determined eyes of

Pippa.

"What's up, love?" Pippa asks, close to Cara's ear.

"I was gonna meet up with you."

Pippa shrugs, her lips tugging into a smile. "I'm here now."

Pippa's arms slide around Cara's waist.

Cara has an immediate reaction to push Pippa away, but something in her gut tells her not to. She takes in the bold and striking features of Pippa's face and can't look away. She pulls her arms around Pippa and moves her body against hers.

Her eyes glue to Pippa's sharp jawline and her lips wet with anticipation.

Pippa pulls in even closer as they dance together, and Cara feels her breath below her ear.

She is so sexy.

Cara's hands run under Pippa's jacket, down her t-shirt, and sit on the top of her leather pants.

Pippa's lips tease Cara's earlobes, and for the first time all night, Cara shuts her eyes. Tingles run down her body and make her toes curl. Cara doesn't hold back as her lips taste Pippa's tantalising jawline.

Pippa combs her fingers through Cara's hair as she angles her head to meet her lips.

Cara kisses Pippa like she's the only thing she's hungry for. She presses her hands against Pippa's back, her t-shirt rides up, and nudges Pippa off the dancefloor. Cara pushes Pippa against the wall and intensifies their kiss.

Pippa bites Cara's lower lip. She pulls out of the kiss, cupping Cara's face in her hands. They stare at one another until Pippa's eyes droop.

Cara dips her shades and stares into Pippa's round, grey eyes.

Pippa's face brightens as she stares into the topaz of Cara's eyes. Cara slides her shades up and kisses the spot below Pippa's jaw. Pippa's hand fishes under Cara's shirt and her fingers tease Cara's skin with tickles.

"Come back to my place," Pippa whispers breathlessly.

Cara runs a hand over Pippa's bust and her knees grow weak. She kisses Pippa's cheek and nods, "Ok."

Pippa locks hands with Cara and pulls herself off the wall. She laughs and then asks, "Did you want your beer? I left our drinks on a table."

Cara doesn't need words to answer when she squeezes Pippa's hand and pulls her towards the door.

Pippa laughs again, happily following Cara out.

They bust into the street, a tangle of hands and lips. Cara slips her hand down the back of Pippa's pants, and Pippa moans in their kiss.

"Ok," Pippa whispers barely out of their kiss. "I've gotta get you home. How dare you still be wearing clothes."

Pippa hails a taxi, and when Cara slides onto the backseat, her gut flips. She desperately wants to share a bed with this girl, but she also really likes her. She's tough and confident. The sexiest qualities in Cara's mind. Whenever she goes home with someone, she uses them for a bed and a shower, and when lucky, also food and money.

She doesn't want to use Pippa.

Before she can commando-roll out of the taxi, Pippa props a finger under her chin, and turns her head to come face-to-face. Pippa's kiss is soft and yet just as passionate as the kisses in the club.

All thoughts of leaving float away as they drive out of the Nightclub District.

The taxi stops at a high-rise apartment complex in Province.

"*Shit*," Cara whispers, looking up at the building. "You live here?"

Pippa smiles and takes Cara's hand, leading her out of the taxi and towards the building. Pippa swipes a card by the front glass doors, and they slide open.

Expose

Cara walks into the foyer with Pippa and her stomach drops. She pulls her hand away and stands still. Usually, an evening in this area of Maiden City feels like a golden ticket. An awesome payday, sending the guy or girl into the bathroom to freshen up, and then taking any cash and small pricey items, and getting the hell out of there.

But this girl is different.

There's something about Pippa that draws Cara in. She doesn't want to rob her.

"What?" Pippa asks in a small voice that's almost fragile.

Cara grits her teeth and swallows hard. She can't bring herself to remove the glasses, but she does one better. "My name is Cara."

Pippa's demeanour softens, and she reaches out her hand again. Cara takes it and they move into the elevator. Pippa stands close, tracing her finger along Cara's jaw and moving it into her hair. The doors ping open and Cara follows to apartment 1606.

When the door opens, the girls connect like magnets. Their hands race into each other's hair, lips mashed together, and explore each other's bodies.

Pippa pushes Cara against the wall, and it's rough and playful like Cara likes.

Cara strips Pippa of her jacket and pulls her t-shirt over her head. She kisses her collarbone and paws over her bra.

Pippa rips off Cara's jacket and moves to her shirt.

She pauses, and it throws Cara off balance. They stare at each other and Pippa's hands raise to Cara's face.

"Why do you hide your face?" Pippa whispers, taking a hold of Cara's dark glasses.

Cara presses against the wall as she allows Pippa to take them off. She closes her eyes, and after two quick breaths, she opens them.

"Your eyes are beautiful," Pippa says, folding the glasses and sitting them on a nearby table.

Cara shifts her clothes, and says, "I'm kinda gross. Mind if I take a shower first?"

A cheeky grin dashes Pippa's lips. She walks backwards, curling her finger for Cara to follow. "Let's scrub up together," she suggests.

Cara laughs and follows Pippa, pulling off her top and unbuttoning her jeans.

Pippa's body is as phenomenal as her tight clothes suggested. Delightfully, there was no deceiving padding in her bra, and her skin is stunningly tanned and glossy under the running water of the shower. They kiss as water cascades between their faces. Cara holds Pippa against her and for a moment forgets the stress that is her life.

Pippa gives her a towel and a robe when they leave the shower. Cara dries her hair as she follows Pippa through the apartment. It's very modern and clean. There is minimal furniture and nothing hanging on the walls except a large television.

"Want a beer?" Pippa asks, pulling open the fridge. "Coffee? Water?"

"Nah, I'm good," Cara says, still taking in the open-plan room.

Pippa walks towards her, drinking from a small bottle of orange juice. "Tired?" she asks, grinning.

Cara pulls Pippa in by her robe's collar and presses her lips against hers.

Pippa nudges to the left. "I'll show you to the bed. I dunno if I'll let you sleep though."

Cara lays her eyes on a double bed. When she crashes, it's just as heavenly soft as expected. The girls lay in each other's arms, listening to the sounds of their happy, exhausted breath.

Cara strokes the wild waves of Pippa's dark hair as her head rests on her shoulder. Holding Pippa, Cara's body is in a state of calm. She looks at the ceiling and around the walls.

Could life be easy?

She rolls onto her side and hugs Pippa tighter.

Could I stay with a girl like this?

Pippa's fingers walk along Cara's spine, creeping towards her head. Her index finger slides along the raised scar at the base of Cara's neck.

"What is that?" Pippa asks, moving to view the back of Cara's neck.

"Nothing!" Cara blurts, pushing away and balancing on the edge of the bed.

"Love," Pippa whispers gently, holding out her hand. "It's ok. I won't look. Come back over. I won't hurt you."

Cara blinks hard at Pippa. A hot pain sizzles through her

forehead as a memory tries to burrow its way out of her subconscious. She rubs her head and huffs as she falls back on the bed.

"You ok?" Pippa whispers, cuddling beside her.

"I've got a monster headache."

"Hangover trying to get you already?"

"Every day is a hangover," Cara grumbles.

Pippa laughs. "You are a party girl."

"No, just nocturnal."

"D'you mind if I catch some *zees*?"

Cara smiles at Pippa and kisses her cheek. "Go for it. I bet you're pretty when you sleep."

Pippa laughs as she yawns. "Either means I'm ugly awake, or you will creepily stare at me when I sleep."

"Way to turn something into a negative."

Pippa grins, eyes closed, and rolls her body against Cara's.

Cara slides her hand down Pippa's back and squeezes her bum. She looks at her face, illuminated by the city light shining in from the window, and smiles.

Yep, beautiful.

Stretching her arms out wide to get comfortable on the bed, Cara's eyes fall on the table by Pippa's bed. Darkened photo frames and canisters sit askew. Cara angles her head to allow the outside lights to expose the items.

Something bronze sits on the table. It's palm size. Curious, Cara narrows her eyes and leans closer.

Pippa moans sleepily, her hands pressing into Cara's waist. "What's wrong?" Pippa mumbles.

Cara gasps. *No way!* She blinks and squints at the object. *A police badge?*

"You're a cop?" Cara accuses, her voice raised.

Pippa pulls herself up, moving to view Cara's face. "Huh?"

Cara points to the object. "What's that badge doing there?"

"I'm a cop, but why are you—"

"—Get off me!" Cara snaps, shoving Pippa away and leaping out of the bed.

"Cara, stop," Pippa says with alarm, scrambling to get out of the bed. "Where are you going? I want you to stay here."

Cara steamrolls as she picks up her clothes from across the apartment. Over the years, she's become exceedingly good at dressing in a hurry. Her jeans are on in one swoop, and her shirt flicks over her head and down her body. She swings her jacket on, snags her glasses, and ignores Pippa's requests for her to calm down and talk to her.

Slipping on her heavy black boots, Cara reefs the front door open and slams it behind her. She runs past the elevator and busts into the fire escape. She has at least a minute up her sleeve. Pippa was still in her robe and Cara assumes she won't run through her apartment building practically naked.

She's a cop? One of those dirty pigs?

How could I be so stupid? How did she fool me so well?

Cara flies down the stairwell and runs into the streets. She runs three blocks and then slows her pace, confident she's zigzagged enough to be off Pippa's radar.

With adrenaline wearing off, her body aches for sleep and her eyes droop. She scuffs her boots into the Nightclub District and eventually makes it to her hideout. Standing by the piles of garbage and wrestling rodents, she pulls out the half-burger from her pocket. She stares at the wrapping and contemplates eating the contents.

Pippa's face clouds her vision.

Anger swells inside her. Her fist crushes the burger.

How could I be so stupid!

She hates herself for slowing down. For letting herself dream of an escape from this life.

Never again.

She tosses the burger on the garbage pile. "I'd rather go hungry."

She picks up a putrid bag of garbage and carries it up the rickety fire escape to her hideout. She hops through the open window and tosses the garbage over the rotting pile already in her abandoned apartment.

Trudging through the mess, she makes her way to the faux wall and opens the hatch. She crawls inside and closes herself into the wall cavity. Her knees pull to her chest and she breathes out, relaxing into being alone. She rests her head against the wall in the hatch and closes her eyes.

Just some sleep and then back to work tomorrow.

Memories

Cara kicks her boot against the faux wall of the hatch. Daylight streams in from the open window and highlights the dump of an apartment. She'll never get used to the stench.

Cara crawls out of the hatch and closes it behind her. She rubs the back of her neck and rolls her shoulders in rough circles. Shaking out her limbs, she makes her way to the window. She sits on the ledge and dangles her legs out and towards the first steps of the rusted fire escape. Blowing out a steady breath, she pulls her glasses from atop her head and sits them on her nose. She folds her arms and sits back, looking over the sullen skyline of the Nightclub District. The area is so gloomy during the day. Without the neon lights and the moving bodies, it's an empty shell of broken people and lost dreams.

With a groan and a stretch of her back, Cara makes it down the stairs and hits the pavement, ready to start her day. A rustling noise grabs her attention, and she moves around the piles of trash to see two girls pilfering the area.

One girl peels back the wrapper of the burger Cara discarded last night. It makes Cara's stomach flip. The girls pick at the burger, huddled together without noticing Cara's presence, despite the clanging she made down the steel steps.

"Hey!" Cara snaps, crossing her arms and jutting her hip.

The girls jolt and break apart, staring at Cara with ajar, burger-filled mouths.

"This my turf," Cara warns. "Piss off!"

The girls stay frozen.

Cara grumbles, rubbing her eyes beneath her dark glasses with heavy pressure. Even the shades can't rid her monster of a headache. She pinches the bridge of her nose, squinting at the girls.

They could definitely be sisters.

Not only their closeness, but their appearances. Seeing kids on the street daily, Cara's unsure whether it is the harsh lifestyle or genetics, but the girls are similarly unattractive. One girl's hair is stark with frizz. Her nose is hooked, her complexion patchy between pale and pink. The other girl's hair is slick with sweat, and her beak nose and forehead are cluttered with acne and scars.

Both girls share the same hunched posture and have rounded eyes which are watery and bloodshot from lack of sleep.

Cara sighs and stomps her foot. "Stop staring at me and leave, would ya?"

"We are just looking for food," Frizzy says.

Sweaty nudges her. "We found food. We are staying here."

"I won't be the fool to judge you," Cara says, turning away from them. "Your foolishness will—"

"—be what judges you," the two girls say in time with Cara.

Cara's chin drops, and she turns back to the girls.

Frizzy points at Cara between the eyes. "Tremaine House!"

Cara backs away. "What?"

The girls stand and step forward. "We're from there too."

"I don't know what you're talking about," Cara says, her voice as shaky as her hands and knees. "You've got the wrong girl."

"You quoted Madam Tremaine," Sweaty says.

Cara's headache intensifies as she tries to stop the slideshow of memories bombarding its way into her brain. "No, I didn't. I don't know why I said that."

"We are your sisters," the girls say in unison.

"*Whoah*," Cara says, taking a mighty leap back. "I ain't anybody's sister."

"We were all sisters at Tremaine House," Frizzy says. "Let us stay with you."

"See the big *steps* I'm taking away from you," Cara says mockingly. "The closest you'll get to me is one giant-step-away sister. I am not your family."

"Just tell us where to go," Frizzy pleads. "If we can't stay here. If we can't go with you. Tell us how to survive."

"I don't take in strays," Cara mutters.

"We're sisters," Sweaty presses. "Look!"

The girl turns her back and pulls down her collar.

"No! Stop," Cara orders, sending her hands out and scrunching her eyes closed. "Don't show me."

Her head sizzles with the familiar pain from the night before.

"I'm Greta," Frizzy says. "And this—"

"—No," Cara blurts. "No names."

"Help us," Greta urges.

"We are not sisters. Get that straight." Cara yells. "I don't care if you were at that place. I have nothing to do with Tremaine."

Greta shoves her sister. "Tell her, Hannah."

Hannah shoves Cara. "What's your name? Tell us."

Cara grounds her boots to keep her balance. "*Geez*, you're aggressive. No, piss off. The only name you get is Girl. You two need to get off my turf five minutes ago."

The sisters' posture deepens into agonising hunches.

Cara huffs, noting their lack of confidence in surviving street life. She steps towards them and digs in her pocket for cash from the last club she visited.

"Take this," Cara says, handing it to one girl. "That's all the help you get. Now scram."

Cara turns and power marches away from the girls and into another alley. She shakes out her shoulders as body tightens. Tension camps along her spine and her hands clamp into fists. Visions of Madam Tremaine crowd her third eye, and Cara wants to scream until she disappears.

Visions of a belt fastening around her neck. A cane whipping her hand in class. Of her bloodied and cut feet after they caught her sneaking out after lights out.

She slaps her head until the memories vanish. Cara hated her time in the foster care system, especially the last government group home, but at least it got her away from Tremaine and eventually to her freedom.

Cara wanders aimlessly as memories seize her mind and try to cripple her. She never reflects on her childhood or what built her into the woman she is today. Never giving the trauma power over her life. She gained her courage and cunning on her own. Nothing will take the ownership away from her.

She meanders through alleys until she's almost at The Limits. She skirts her way around the edge of the barren and underprivileged area of the city. Slowing her pace, she enters another alley. She holds her breath as she realises where her subconscious has taken her while she was busy ridding childhood memories from her mind.

The place where she gained her freedom.

Where she helps others escape.

The place she made a home for her and the person she loved the most. Adrian.

She looks down the alley and a curly mop of brown hair ducks and weaves, belonging to a boy she helped a few months ago. He hides behind two other people. A girl with red hair, and another boy.

Adrian.

Adrian, her brother, stands and looks directly at her.

"Cara!" he calls out.

Cara runs.

She runs away, into another alley and back towards the heart of the Nightclub District.

I left for a reason. I can't hurt him again. Why did I go back there?

Shit.

Her breathing and heart rate slows as she approaches the Youth Hostel. She walks through the side entrance and meets Julius in his office.

"Hey Girl," Julius says, reclining on his office chair and gives her a wave. "You not been around in a while."

"Had to lay low," Cara replies. "You got work for me?"

"Bathroom pipes all busted again," Julius says.

Cara's eyebrows raise and she winces. "As bad as last time?"

Julius smiles. "So-so."

"That's a yes if I ever heard one," Cara mutters.

"What you want for payment? A bed or food?"

"Food. Can you get Rod to leave it out the back for me? I'll pick it up when I'm done."

"No problemo. Tools are where you left them."

Cara nods and walks to the back maintenance closet. A navy baseball cap sits on a hook where she left it. She puts it on and tucks her hair inside. She changes out of her bomber jacket and throws on grey, grease-stained overalls. Lugging her toolkit out of the closet, she hobbles her way to the communal bathrooms.

As she gets to work on a pipe under a basin, she listens to two girls who freshen up before tonight's work. Obvious strip club workers, evident by the hair extensions, body glitter, and the self-loathing etched on their faces.

Nothing like the confident and tough Pippa.

Cara's insides contort.

A cop. A no good, stinking cop!

It's well known on the streets to never trust law enforcement. The rules change by the minute. Hell, they'd arrest you for taking a nap in the wrong place.

Two young men walk out of the male area and whisper gruffly at each other. Sores cover their arms and faces. Their hair is matted and dull. Cara takes a mental note to inform a Neon there are new people here to sell to.

Cara works on some shower drains, and Julius advises her the toilet by his office is leaking.

Eww. He clogged it, the big oaf.

She tells Julius to triple her food payment and find her a new set of clothes, hardly worn.

After finishing the doozy of manual labour dumped on her today, she takes the opportunity for a quick shower. Keeping her head down and eyes shaded, she leaves the hostel through the kitchen, dressed in her new clothes and trusty bomber jacket.

"Mayor keeps talking about shutting down The Limits," Rod says, tapping at the radio where a news broadcast just came through.

"And where the hell those people gonna go?" the other cook says.

"They got money, they can have a cot here," Rod says.

"That's all this area needs. More gangbangers selling pills and streetwalkers turning tricks."

Cara takes her overloaded food package and leaves the men continuing their conversation. She doesn't know if they saw her and frankly couldn't care less.

Cara moves down an alley, lifting her food package high.

"I love a girl who comes bearing gifts," a sultry voice calls from the shadows.

A curvy Latina with black and neon green hair, braided at the side, walks towards her. Her hands sit in the pockets of her Neon leather jacket, her skirt hugs her thighs, her black boots cover her calves, and her visible tattoos run along her neck and under the holes of her fishnet stockings.

"Let's call it a peace offering," Cara replies.

A tall man with dark skin, almond eyes, and bright purple hair, walks by his Neon partner.

Kaz makes working with the Neons bearable, but her partner

Raif I can live without.

Raif walks up to her and snatches the food parcel. "You got names for us, or what?"

"Thirteen fresh faces down at the Youth Hostel," Cara says, grabbing the food parcel. "But I get my share of the food first."

Kaz pats Raif's shoulder. "You check out the hostel. I wanna talk with Girl for a minute."

Raif looks her up and down. "You going sweet on this one?"

"Just go," Kaz orders. She nods at Cara. "Where should he look?"

"Two guys on the first level dorms. Three girls are new to working the strip clubs, so maybe you wanna get them after their shift. I saw six hanging around the bathrooms, already into some stuff so it'll be an easy transaction. And another two guys, I'm not sure if they were staying there or just passing through. It's been a while since I was last there, so it's ripe for the picking."

Raif stands an inch from Cara and breathes heavily over her face. He flicks the glass of her dark shades and grimaces at her. He then pushes past and stomps down the alley.

Cara nods to Kaz, holding the food high. "You gotta let Dean know I'm making up for lost time. Give me some breathing room away from him."

"You always get yourself into trouble, Girl," Kaz says, sitting on a box by the dumpster. "Few people have the King on their tale. He took a shine to you."

"Well, I don't want his shine. He can find someone else to linger over."

"Why don't you just join us?" Kaz asks. "You're as good as in."

"I'm not one for teammates," Cara says, taking some fries. "I prefer to lone wolf things."

"I heard he poached your haul last night."

"Last night was rough, to say the least."

"You back to work tonight?"

"Yeah. I'm gonna try the Samsonite Club."

"Nice. I'll join you."

"What did I say about me and teammates?"

"Girl, I ain't no pickpocket. I'm there to get drunk." Kaz winks, pulling out a handful of fries. "And maybe watch ya work."

Cara stuffs her face with food, trying to ignore Kaz. She used to crush hard on Kaz, but she's a tease. A straight girl leading her on for her own gain. She's Cara favourite Neon to give information to, but it's coming time to find someone else to work with. Cara doesn't want her emotions getting in the way, especially after the disaster that ended last night.

A cop. I slept with a cop. Disgusting!

After they eat and stash the food in an abandoned storage room, Cara and Kaz move onto Samsonite. A club heavy on electro sounds, mind-altering light effects, and a deep pocket crowd.

Kaz walks ahead, flipping her collar up and parting the crowd with her attitude. She lands at the bar and pounds on the tabletop, ordering a double whisky.

"Girl, what you getting?" Kaz yells over the noise.

"Later," Cara says, moving away. "Alone, remember?"

Kaz glares at the server pouring her drink too slow for her liking. The crowd around the bar moves as one away from her. She kicks back on a stool, surveying the area, and Cara is more than glad she's in Kaz's good books tonight.

Cara shimmies through the dancefloor, head down, eyeing the array of pockets before her. Again, she needs to replenish her cash pile, having paid off the two girls earlier outside her hideout. The last month seems to have worked collectively to keep Cara behind. Every time she collects a decent haul, someone takes it from her. If things keep going this way, she'll end up in The Limits for good.

Cara slides around a few couples, dipping into their back pockets. She finds cash and slips off bracelets. She figures she'll move onto another club so Kaz doesn't steal tonight's haul from her.

While picking from a few more people, maniacal shrieks and cheers sound on the dancefloor. Cara looks around and is shocked to see the two Tremaine girls from earlier, jumping in front of people and grabbing at their belongings.

They jump in front of Cara, whose annoyance gets the better of her, and she yells, "What are you two doing?"

"We're making money!" Greta cheers. She wolf-whistles and throws herself at people, trying for intimidating.

"Hand over your cash, Girl," Hannah orders Cara, punching her shoulder.

"*Oi!*" Cara shouts, rubbing her shoulder. "What the hell you robbing me for?"

"I seen you taking from others here," Hannah counters.

Cara looks around, the crowd now aware of them thanks to Greta throwing herself in their faces.

Dammit. I've been made.

Cara turns to flee the club, but Hannah grabs her jacket.

"Gimme the money!" she yells.

"Let go of me you, you waste of space!" Cara yells, thrashing against Hannah's grip.

Hannah lets go when Kaz grabs her by the neck and yanks her backwards. Hannah yelps as she's dragged away from Cara.

"No teammates, huh?" Kaz questions.

"They are not with me," Cara blurts, agitated. "I gotta get out of here."

Kaz steps in front of Cara, her eyes glowing with determination. "We use you because you're invisible. You lose that you're useless. When you're useless, we no longer give you your space."

"They're not with me," Cara repeats, a pleading in her tone.

Kaz shoves her. "Get out of here before I see anything I need to report."

Cara grits her teeth and hands clench into fists. "Don't tell Dean anything. This wasn't my fault."

Cara turns and leaves before Kaz changes her mind.

She hits the street, and two sets of erratic footsteps follow her.

You've got to be kidding me.

She turns and the two manic sisters are on her tale.

"Stop following me," Cara calls. "You ruined everything back there."

"I figured, why rob everyone else when you can do it for us," Hannah says, a disturbing grin creasing her face.

"You could just teach us," Greta says, leaning on her sister. "Then we wouldn't get in your way."

"No matter what, you two would always be in the way. What was that in there? You got every single person's attention. You can't pickpocket if people see you."

"Who was that woman? How come she gets to hang with you?"

Cara deadpans. "The neon hair didn't tip you off? You know this in gang territory, right?"

"We're our own gang," Hannah says proudly.

Cara blows a raspberry. "I don't see you two surviving a second."

"That's why we are roping you in," Greta says. "Work with us."

"Working with the Neons is survival," Cara says in a low tone. "I can't lose their trust, and in thirty seconds you almost blew up a year's hard work."

Hannah spits phlegm on the pavement. "Whatever."

"We are sisters," Greta blurts with passion. "We should stick together."

"You gotta learn on your own. Madam Tremaine was heavy on chores and education. She taught you how to focus and learn by observing. She made us do physical labour, so use it to make money." Cara huffs and turns away from the pair. "Use something to your advantage. Just don't use me."

"We should just take like you do," Hannah grumbles. "Then you just bow down to those gang members."

"I work with the Neons and they let me keep my turf in the District," Cara tells. "I'm not letting you two ruin everything. You wanna steal from people, be my guests, but leave me the hell alone."

A siren fires behind Cara. Over her shoulder appears the flash of blue and red lights.

Shit. Cops.

Someone inside Samsonite must have narked.

Without another moment wasted on these two girls, Cara flees on foot. Away from them and the cops, and towards the safety of

The Limits.

35

Glitter

Caden Walsh reclines on his deck chair, watching the water lap by his yacht. Everyone refers to him by his full name, and why wouldn't they? His last name is the part that matters. The part that gives him prestige and privilege. There's a high school in Hamlet bearing his name, streets throughout Province named after his family, and three buildings at his university dedicated to his family members.

He reflects on his last day of school before his island-hopping vacation. His economics profession spoke to him about his grades slipping, and alluded to plagiarism and accusations about cheating.

One phone call to his father washed away his problems. Another cheque written. Another plaque on a wall. Another time Caden's actions meant absolutely nothing.

But it gave him an idea. He can pay off people himself. Why wait for the fallout? He lined up students to write his upcoming assignments and got his payroll sorted. As they busily work on his projects and turn them in via his student portal log in, he uses the time to party and enjoy the finer things in life.

Hopefully, he'll never talk to another teacher again.

I wonder how many of them I can get on the payroll before I enrol for next semester's classes.

He stretches out, and the sun warms his coconut-oiled body. His six-pack abs glisten and he dips his sunglasses to wink at the bikini-clad girls, giggling at him by the bubbling hot tub.

His butler places a freshly-made tropical cocktail on a nearby table. Caden takes it and saunters over to the girls.

"Having fun ladies?" Caden asks, showing off his charisma-soaked smile.

The girls giggle and beckon him over. They slip into the hot, rapid water.

Caden sinks in between the girls, gasping an *ahh* sound as he acclimatises to the water's temperature. With pleasure, he ogles their perky bust sizes and jaw-dropping cleavages.

One girl tosses her arm around Caden's neck and slides onto his lap. She kisses the nape of his neck as his hand plays at the string tied across her back.

The other girl slides up to his ear and whispers, "What about me?"

Caden grins, and instantly the girl's lips press onto his.

"Partying without us?" Caden's friend, Henry, calls out. He and the other two lads slide into the large square hot tub.

The girl, who had her lips on Caden, wades over to Tyler and slings her arms around him. She nibbles at his earlobe.

"Clements," Caden calls to his butler. "Can you go below deck and get the other girls out of bed?"

"I'll check on them, Sir," Clements replies with a nod.

"They're totally passed out," the girl on Caden's lap says with a giggle.

Caden looks over her shoulder to Derek. "How much stuff did you give them?"

Derek swats a hand, looking out to the sea. "Don't stress, man. They'll be up in no time."

"What good is it having the girls outnumber us," Tyler says, "if all but two are passed out?"

"We'll dock at another island tonight," Henry says. "We'll pick up more girls there."

Caden pushes the girl off his lap and huffs. "I'm bored with the islands. I want to get back to the city and to the strip clubs."

"Dude, that means crashing at the frat house," Tyler grizzles. "I need to lay low after what happened at the last party."

"We can come back to the boat," Caden replies. "I'm just so bored. I want to play poker while getting a lapdance."

"We can organise that to come to us," Derek says.

Caden slides further into the water. "*Boring.*"

The lads laugh, and Henry says, "We better head back tonight. We all know how whiny Caden gets when he's bored."

Caden pulls himself out of the hot tub. "I'll tell the Skipper to turn back. In the meantime, I'll tend to the ladies downstairs."

"Want a teammate?" Tyler calls, sporting a devilish grin.

Caden smirks. "I got it. I'll tag you in later."

Leaving the girls to find their own way home, the lads follow Caden into Cherry Stems Club. Caden soaks in the familiar scent of body oil, scotch, and hormones. The black walls and red vinyl booths make him feel at home. A spotlight hits the catwalk, and he grins at the many brass poles awaiting the scintillating performers.

The lads get a table by the catwalk. Caden pulls his chair out and sits wide-legged, ready for someone to take up residence on his lap. He holds cash in the air, and in a matter of seconds, four barely clothed ladies crowd their table.

Henry grins at a girl straddling him. His hands raise to touch her, but he stops and looks over his shoulder. He groans and says to Caden, "This sucks. On the yacht we could touch the girls."

"Calm down," Caden says. "We can touch these girls too, just not out here with the paupers."

Caden smiles at the beauty swaying her hips in front of him. Her dark skin glows with gold glitter, and her black and bronze lingerie fits her curvy figure to perfection. Her long braids swish around her body as she dances.

He lifts a wad of cash and says to her, "We'd like a private room with the best dealer and more girls like you."

The girl leans over and whispers, "As you wish."

Caden tucks the cash inside her lingerie, and she takes him by the hand, the lads avidly following.

Caden floats as he is escorted into the back, where the private rooms and large gambling areas are. His smile won't leave his face until...

"Caden, my boy!" his father's voice calls out.

Caden's gut plummets to the floor and he turns to the right, where his father beckons him over from a private room. Two girls perform a striptease in front of him, and Caden doesn't want the visual imprinted on his brain.

His father stands, his tie and most of his shirt undone, and moves to the doorway of his private room. "I thought you were island hopping."

"Wanted a change of scenery," Caden replies.

"No better place," his father says with a chuckle. He nods to the girl attached to Caden's hand. "Angelina is one of the best. Nice choice."

Ugh, shut up, Dad.

"Mr W," Derek says. "Your door was wide open. Aren't you worried about people peeping on you?"

Mayor Walsh smiles and pulls cash from his pocket. "Not when silence is for sale." He holds the money towards Derek. "Right lads? This stays between us."

"We won't tell anyone," Tyler is quick to respond, eyes on the wad.

Caden's father pays off his friends, and Caden eagerness for poker and a lapdance dwindles.

"C'mon, baby," Angelina says, tugging on Caden's hands. "We're ready for you."

"Go get 'em, Son," Mayor Walsh says, patting Caden on the back and then returning to his room.

Ugh.

Caden follows Angelina and plans to lay down the biggest bet of his life. Why not? It is his father's money, after all.

Innocent

Pippa can't stop thinking about her. The moment she saw the colour of Cara's eyes was like magic.

Cara ran because she saw my badge.

Pippa closes the door to her locker outside the police station's gym, and makes her way upstairs to her desk. An ugly pain clamps her gut. The same pain she feels when thinking about the corruption plaguing Maiden City. The corruption that made her become a cop, and made Cara run.

She thinks I'm one of them. A dirty cop. I need to find her. I need to explain I'm not like that. That I'm on the force to work from the inside out.

At her desk, Pippa logs onto the computer. She searches through the records for incidents in the Nightclub District. She skims through witnesses, potential suspects, and bystanders looking for physical descriptions matching Cara's.

She finds references to a blonde woman with dark glasses and notes the case file numbers. She searches for "Cara" but soon finds a first name is not enough to go on. Cases from the past decades slow down her search speed.

That mark.

Cara had a raised marking between her shoulders. The thought of me seeing it terrified her.

Pippa's fingers rub together as she recalls it feeling like a T, and it wasn't so much a scar, but maybe… a burn?

Pippa searches keywords to help discover Cara's identity. Clicking a few results, and typing different phrases, Pippa finds the Tremaine case. A former foster home. *The Tremaine House for Troubled Girls.*

Pippa's stomach squeezes. Reading the report, she learns the home was shut down after multiple allegations of child abuse.

Oh shit.

When Pippa reads, "they branded the girls with a T between their shoulder blades," her breakfast launches into her throat.

This is barbaric. Was that mark a Tremaine branding? Did Cara live at this place?

Pippa keeps clicking, finding records of the girls homed at Tremaine House. Scanning the list of names, Pippa lands on *Cara Tremaine.*

Tremaine? Was Cara a blood relative? What does this mean? I need to find her and make sure she's ok.

Deciding to go off the vague descriptions of the blonde with dark glasses, Pippa writes the cross streets mentioned in the reports and will visit the areas while on patrol.

Fitzpatrick walks into the station, sipping coffee from a paper cup as his eyes droop into the dark bags, ageing his scruffy face.

"Morning, Jackson," he says in a gravelly tone.

"Morning Fitz. Rough night last night?"

Fitzpatrick sits at the adjacent desk with a groan and a cough. "You could say that."

Pippa casually jots down Fitz's time of arrival and his demeanour in her notebook. She is still unsure of his dealings with corruption at the station. At this point, everyone is a suspect until proven innocent. The evidence she is collecting is stacking up. Straight-laced police officers are yielding to the appeal of money. It starts with letting a CEO's teenager get away with a joyride, or miss-marking an evidence bag so it's useless at trial. Every phone call or bribe snowballs into a bigger injustice.

No wonder the citizens are so distrustful of police officers. Especially those in the lower-class districts.

Her mind goes back to Cara. Her badass attitude. Her effortless movements.

Pippa spotted her right away attempting to rob people in the club. *And she was damn good at it. I'd just rather give her the money to make sure she ate.*

She thinks of Cara's body when they were in the shower together. Her ribs were prominent, and skin was rough in places. She wasn't eating disorder skinny. She was *poor* skinny.

I need to find her. I want to make sure she's safe. I need her to be safe.

"What ya working on?" Fitz asks, popping two ibuprofens.

"Oh, nothing really," Pippa says, closing out the case files on her screen. "Had a hunch on something, but it was probably nothing."

Fitz reclines in his seat, clicking his tongue as he cranes his neck to view her computer monitor. "Talk it out. Maybe I can help."

Pippa gets up from her seat, tightening her ponytail. "No, it's ok. I was going around in circles." She points to Fitz's paper cup. "I need one of those. Excuse me."

Fitzpatrick raises the cup with a smirk. "No problem."

Pippa walks towards the break room, stretching her arms over her head. Suddenly her gym session feels like days ago, instead of only 30 minutes. No longer invigorated, she feels tight and knotted.

As she pours herself a coffee, more of her colleagues enter the station. Some have phones glued to their ears, others are scribbling into notepads, or logging into their computers. Pippa has notes on everyone. Some she has hard proof of their dirty dealings, and others have come up empty. None proven innocent, yet. She hopes some come up clean. It can't just be her.

She dumps sugar into her coffee, knowing she needs more of an energy boost than just the caffeine can provide. She mulls on how she might react if a high-ranking government official asked her to ignore a crime committed. Or asked her to conduct an illegal wiretap. Her ethics would never allow her to engage in something like that, but how would she tell them no? Most government officials outrank her. How does she go against their wishes and not get fired? If she gets fired, then all of this is for nothing. How can she help erase corruption from Maiden City if she's kicked off the force?

She walks back to her desk, slurping the sugary beverage, when she spies Fitzpatrick hovering over her desk.

"Lose something?" she asks, scanning her desk for what he's looking for.

"A pen that works," he grumbles. He scribbles something down and then says, "C'mon, we gotta go. Domestic dispute in

Hamlet."

Pippa grabs her jacket as she asks, "Anyone we know?"

"Williams' house on Perry Street."

Pippa eyes her desk and sees her notebook open, face down, and askew. She didn't leave it like that. Either Fitz moved it when looking for a pen… or he was snooping through it.

Pippa picks up the notebook and slides it into her pocket, following Fitz out towards the parking lot.

"I've been out there before," Fitzpatrick says as they head for the patrol car. "Neighbours witness the old man beating his wife and kid. Same thing every time. He yells at us to leave and she denies anything bad happening."

"And the kid?" Pippa asks, bracing for the answer.

"I think he's out of the picture."

Pippa's blood runs cold. "Dead or runaway?"

"Runaway, I believe."

"Lord, another kid on the streets. This city is going to the pits."

"And that's why we need to clean it up."

"Clean it up? You sound like the Mayor."

"I'll take that as a compliment."

"I'm obviously not going to bad mouth our boss, but there's more to do than cosmetic fixes. These kids have no place to go. There needs to be more help. Like education for households, mental health support, and financial aid."

"A bleeding-heart cop. Never thought I'd see the day."

"I care about the people in this city. I love this city and don't want to see it in ruins."

"Then be glad Bradford Walsh is in charge. He's going to make Maiden City better than it's ever been."

Pippa stays silent on the matter as they drive into Hamlet, the working-class area of Maiden City. She makes a mental note of Fitzpatrick quoting Mayor Walsh. She's also anxious over the fact he snooped through her notes. Internally, she scolds herself. She should know better than to make notes on colleagues in a paper form anyone can pick up. She just couldn't have it on her work computer, and she is used to taking notes by hand. It's something she picked up early, and it has always stuck.

"I can't do this anymore!" a woman screams on the front lawn as the patrol car pulls up at the house.

When the car comes to a stop, Pippa launches out of the car. She raises her hands and edges toward the woman.

"Ma'am?" Pippa begins. "Are you all right? I'm Officer Jackson, and behind me is Officer Fitzpatrick. We are here to help."

Fitzpatrick approaches behind Pippa. With her peripheral vision, she witnesses Fitz's hand tap his holster.

"I can't live in this house anymore!" the woman screeches.

"Mrs Williams, is your husband home?" Fitzpatrick asks, taking a wide berth around her.

"Sitting on the sofa like he always does," Mrs Williams says, her face red and eyes filled with tears.

Fitzpatrick moves towards the house, calling for Mr Williams.

Pippa moves closer to Mrs Williams. "Ma'am, has he hurt you?"

"He won't let my son come back," she whimpers. "We're always arguing about it."

"Your son? Where is he?"

"He moved out."

"Do you know where he is?"

Mrs Williams lifts her shaking hand, and crumpled in her tight fist, is a card. "He won't let me go there and visit him."

"It's a foster home?"

"I want my son back!" Mrs Williams cries and her knees buckle.

"Ma'am!" Pippa catches Mrs Williams before she falls.

"I made a big mistake," she whispers.

Pippa stands the woman upright. "Tell me what has happened."

"I sided with my husband. I lost my son."

"Your husband abused your son?"

Mrs Williams sniffles and nods her head.

Pippa jots some notes in her notebook.

Mrs Williams holds out the card. "This is the address where Gene lives."

"Gene? That's your son's name?"

"Yes."

"How old?"

"Fifteen."

Pippa writes the address and the boy's details in her notebook. She looks at the phone number on the card and questions the name next to it.

"Jazz Abadi? The heiress?"

"She's the woman who helped Gene move out."

"Jackson," Fitzpatrick calls as he exits the house. "Let's get going."

As Fitz walks through the front yard, Pippa gains eye contact with Mrs Williams. "Do you feel safe here?"

"I'll wait here for my son," Mrs Williams says, and turns back to the house.

"Jackson. Move it," Fitzpatrick calls from the car.

With tight shoulders, Pippa returns to the car. When no accusation of spousal abuse comes forward, Pippa's hands are tied. She enters the car with Fitzpatrick and feels useless.

"Don't send yourself crazy trying to help every depressed housewife. It's a never-ending list," Fitzpatrick says as they drive down the street.

"It's the kid I'm worried about."

"Don't waste your time following that up. If you want to do something, call social services and have someone update his file. You saw how high-strung the mother was. He's probably out of there for a reason."

"I didn't get to see the husband. What kind of state was he in?"

"He didn't seem inebriated," Fitzpatrick tells. "But he was surly. Didn't want cops on the premises for sure."

"Another civilian to not trust cops?"

"I think it was more a privacy issue. Seemed like a prideful man." Fitzpatrick glances in Pippa's direction. "Leave this one alone, Jackson. We did our job."

Pippa understands what Fitz is saying perfectly clear. The Mayor has a lot of business interests in Maiden City. The families in Hamlet work for the upper-class elite, whose best interests are to not have the abuse and depression of their worker's home lives broadcast as common knowledge.

If there's no bloodshed, keep it quiet.

Child

Gene feels gross. All he wanted was some excitement and fun. But gross is all he got.

Maybe it's not even that. As he scuffs his feet through the hall of the shelter, he feels low. His head tilts down, his shoulders curve over, and his stomach plummets lower than it should.

He spent last night in the Nightclub District. He left the shelter late at night, and his roommates were sound asleep.

He's spent more nights than he cares to admit, wandering that area in search of some attention. It now feels like an addiction. It doesn't leave him feeling good, but he can't stop. Every time he tells himself that next time will be better. The next time he'll find his perfect person, or at least an hour of romance. He hopes...

In his attempt to cruise guys last night, he dressed in his best outfit and spent too long styling his hair to perfection. He lent against the wall of nightclubs, fake-ID-less, and hid in darkness when gang members strolled by. He tried to talk to oh-so-gorgeous men, but they looked at him sideways. They saw him as a child. Like he didn't belong. Like a poser.

He dragged himself home like a total loser. He has nothing else to try. All around him, couples spring up out of nowhere. He hates admitting he is jealous, but everywhere he turns, it's in his face. He shares a room with Max, who is constantly cuddling up with Tessa from down the hall. Eddy and Aria are about the most adorable thing he's ever seen. And it happened like magic. An instant connection.

This morning he plonks himself down at a table in the dining room for breakfast and hangs his head in his hands.

"Morning, Genie," the best voice in the world says.

He looks up and is instantly smiling. Smiling back at him is Adrian.

Adrian.

Any storm cloud that strikes his day is always thwarted by the sunshine that is Adrian.

"Good morning," he replies.

"Sleep ok?" Adrian asks, leaning on the back of a plastic chair.

Gene gazes into Adrian's eyes like he's the only person in the room. He nods and says, "Like a baby."

Jazz walks up behind Adrian and slings her arms around his shoulders and nuzzles her face by his.

"Hey Gene," she says sweetly.

"Hi," Gene replies.

Gene loves Jazz, but she's really great at shattering his illusions.

Can't she just give me one minute with Adrian and my imagination?

Gene knows in his heart he doesn't want Adrian romantically, but he's the closest to a real relationship he's got. Adrian and Jazz's relationship is sublime, and Gene commends himself for having a hand in getting the two together. He just didn't realise at the time that it would feed his jealousy.

Romance hasn't come easy for him. Taking matters into his own hands gives him strength. He won't be the scared boy anymore. The one who hid in his bedroom at his parents' house, scrolling through social media and daydreaming about another life. When he moved out of their house, he vowed to live his life. No secrecy. No hiding who he is.

His stomach jitters as he thinks over last night's actions. The secrecy. His eyes wander over Adrian. In his heart, he knows he'd never be able to admit to Adrian what he's doing. He couldn't stand the disappointment looking back at him. Not from such beautiful brown eyes.

Stop it, Gene.

He rubs his forehead in frustration.

"What's wrong?" Adrian asks.

Gene drops his hand and meets Adrian's eyes. They are full of warm concern.

Gene smiles. "Nothing. Just thinking about a homework assignment."

"Do you need any help?" Jazz offers.

"No, it's ok. I'm sure Adrian is keeping you busy with the tutoring."

Adrian sighs, grinning. "Don't bring it up."

Jazz and Adrian smile and laugh together.

Gene can't help being happy and jealous all in one neatly dressed parcel.

Ego

Pippa fixes her badge proudly onto her pristine navy blue uniform. Her uniform is always pristine at the start of her shift, but she can't speak for the end of her shift.

She takes the elevator and moves through the rows of desks to her own. She's an hour early for her shift, so the night crew is crashing in the break room or still coming back from patrol. Her crew isn't as punctual as her. Except for her Captain.

Captain McNeil strides past her desk and taps it with rolled up paperwork.

"My office," he says as he marches away from Pippa.

"Yes, Sir," Pippa is quick to reply, bounding out of her chair and following the Captain to his office.

"Shut the door behind you," the Captain orders as he moves behind his desk.

"Sure," she says, finding it odd when the floor is empty. She closes the door and sits on the chair in front of the Captain's desk.

"You have a new assignment," the Captain begins.

Pippa sits tall, perching on the edge of her seat. "Great," she replies. "Shouldn't we wait for my partner to get here?"

"Fitzpatrick won't be joining you," Captain McNeil says with a stony face. "And you won't be reporting to me."

"I don't understand." Pippa still finds it hard to read her Captain.

"You're being moved to the Mayor's security detail."

"Excuse me?" Pippa splutters. "You want me to be a security guard?"

"It's not my call," Captain McNeil says, pushing papers towards Pippa. "You had to know this was coming."

"What? Because I was questioning Ignacio's motives?" Pippa says, agitated.

"And poking around in the evidence lockers and files."

"Poking around?" Heat rises from her collar. "It's called doing my job."

"Jackson, it's not negotiable. You are to report to Lieutenant Byrne in thirty minutes at Walsh Mansion."

Pippa stands, swiping the paperwork from the Captain's desk. "I've been a good cop. All I want is justice and truth for this city."

"Maybe you'll find what you're looking for in your new position."

Pippa huffs and storms out of the office. She contemplates that she probably shouldn't walk out on her commanding officer in such a tizzy, but she is pissed. The Mayor's security detail is a slap in the face.

A shit-kicker position.

She has questioned corruption within the force and tried to gain answers to confirm her suspicions. Ignacio is a crooked cop, leaving trails of evidence everywhere he goes. Any cop doing half a job can see it.

Is McNeil part of it? Is he crooked?

She grabs her jacket and moves back to her locker for her wallet and keys. Maybe working closely to the Mayor could be good for her career, but not when she's in the middle of a personal investigation.

Maybe if I get close enough to him, I can discuss cleaning up politics and law enforcement. But I can already tell it will fall on deaf ears.

On the drive to Walsh Mansion in Sovereign Hill, Pippa reflects on why she became a cop. Her new position makes her blood boil. Her grip on the steering wheel is so intense that her knuckles whiten, her fingers pulse red, and a heavy sweat builds in her palms.

When Pippa moved back to Maiden City, she vowed to help the people. The police force was the perfect fit. When she finished her training and was assigned under Captain McNeil, things seemed off. Officers had assignments they weren't reporting back to the Captain. Many hushed phone calls, conducted hunched over desk phones or running to the nearest alcove. Officers would rush out of the station on a job they couldn't discuss. Not every job is top secret. If you're busting a junkie for selling on a street corner, you can tell the cop at the adjacent desk.

Pippa brakes at the large wrought-iron gate and pushes the buzzer on an intercom.

"Yeah?" a gruff voice answers.

"Officer Jackson, reporting for duty."

"Come through."

The gates open and Pippa exhales a steady breath as she drives the long path to Walsh Mansion.

She smooths down her uniform as she gets out of the car and

makes her way to the front door. The door opens, and she's greeted by what looks like another rookie cop.

"Jackson," she introduces herself with a nod.

"Deacon," he replies, and nudges for her to enter.

As Pippa enters the foyer, she's smacked in the face with the lavishness. The huge teardrop crystal chandelier, blindingly sparkling tile floors, and expensive furniture with even more expensive items sitting atop them.

"I'll take you to Byrne," Officer Deacon says, marching ahead of her.

Pippa follows, scanning every inch of the rooms they pass.

"You're Jackson?" a man says brashly, slamming down a phone.

"Yes, Sir," Pippa replies, assuming this is Lieutenant Byrne.

"*Dammit.* Did you just get out of the academy? Can they stop sending me mouseketeers?"

"I'm a good cop," Pippa replies, standing tall. "Whatever you need, I will excel at it."

"Another ego," Byrne says. "Like this house isn't already full of that." He points to Deacon. "Show her to the north wing. Jackson, you'll shadow Deacon today. I got enough to worry about with this stupid Ball approaching. Like I've got nothing better to do."

"Yes, Sir," Pippa and Deacon reply in unison.

Pippa follows Deacon out and wonders what her job will entail. She didn't expect a Lieutenant to talk like that. He sounded like an angry party planner, not an officer on the force.

"He's talking about the Masquerade Ball coming up," Deacon says as they walk a long hallway.

"Oh yeah. The Mayor holds it every year, right?"

"Right. That's why we have extra security on. To get ready for the event."

"Do they have intel on an upcoming attack?" Pippa's enthusiasm piques at the possibility of taking down a terrorist.

"Not to my knowledge."

Pippa's excitement sinks.

"The Mayor requested more bodies, so that's what he got."

"There must be something big happening," Pippa deduces.

"Oh, why hello there," a voice says from the nearby winding staircase.

A wildly handsome man sails down the stairs, and Pippa instantly recognises him. *Caden Walsh, the Mayor's son.*

"Finally," Caden says, walking towards them. "An officer I can lay my eyes on." He extends his hand to Pippa. "Caden Walsh. Lovely to meet you."

Pippa shakes his hand out of formality. "Officer Jackson. Glad to be of service."

Caden wets his lips. "What I like to hear."

Pippa looks to Deacon. "You were showing me to the north wing?"

"Right." Deacon nods. "Excuse us, Mr Walsh."

"Leaving already?" Caden says, looking Pippa up and down. "If you need a tour upstairs, you come and find me."

"Don't worry yourself, Mr Walsh," Pippa says. "I'm here to protect you. Not the other way round."

Caden eyes her bum as they pass. "I'll be seeing you around, Officer Jackson."

"It's my job to be here, Mr Walsh," Pippa says bluntly, as she follows Deacon along the hall.

"Don't sound so thrilled," Caden calls with a boyish laugh.

"If you're going to sleep with him, try to do it off the clock," Deacon says.

Pippa gasps with a mixture of shock and disgust. "I would never do something so abhorrent!"

"You don't need to get defensive," Deacon says, unlocking a door. "Caden Walsh has a very high success rate. You can sleep with him, but don't let it affect the rest of your duties."

"The *rest* of my duties?" Pippa says as a rage builds inside her. She slams her hand on the door to gain Deacon's full attention. "You say that like it's my female duty to submit to any man who wants my body. Don't you dare speak to me like that again. It is not my duty to give my body to anyone, no matter their title."

"Hey, don't get huffy with me," Deacon says, turning the doorknob and reefing the door to remove Pippa's hand. "Do your hormones always affect your job?"

"Do yours?" Pippa asks with outrage.

She lets Deacon walk into the room and buries her emotions. Not a good look to smash her colleague's head on the first day.

Great. Another misogynist dirtbag to add to my investigation.

"This is our break room," Deacon says, gesturing to the narrow room. "It's for cops and security only. You can leave belongings in here, and it's a shortcut between wings. If you'll follow me through this door at the other end, I'll show you to your post."

"Post? Does that mean I just stand and watch?"

"Precisely."

"Watch for what? What is the Mayor expecting to happen here?"

"You keep looking for some big mystery. It's an appearance thing. Haven't you worked out these elitists yet? He needs bodies guarding him to appear as powerful as possible."

Deacon shows her along the northern hallway, the upstairs library and parlour, the balcony, and below to the rose gardens. He tells her to stay by the staircase and keep watch.

For the first time, Pippa hates her job.

Of course, they put me on this assignment. I'm paralysed. I can't investigate, and I can't leave. I'm told where to stand and what I can watch.

They know I'm on to them. This confirms I was right. Fitz read my notes and ratted me out.

I must use this place to my advantage. That is, if I don't fall asleep first.

Facade

Jazz cheers a *whoop* as she and Adrian make their way into his room at the shelter, after their run. She smiles at the slick sweat in his hair, and the way he fans out his muscle shirt. It shows off how hard he pushed. His lean limbs have tone to them, now that they've been working out together for a few months.

Jazz feels her muscles tingle as her body cools down. She stretches out in her black sports bra and leggings.

"Come here," he says, smiling, and pulls her into a hug.

She enjoys leaning against him in her tight and revealing clothing, knowing someday soon she will get even closer to this man she loves. She kisses him soft and slow, her energy drained from their workout.

When they pull apart, Adrian crashes onto his bed and blows out a drained breath. "I'm just gonna take a minute before heading to the showers."

Jazz sits next to him and taps the notecards and small books she'd left with him. "How's the reading coming along?"

Adrian grizzles. "Not well."

"You were doing well with this one," Jazz says, lifting a book, but Adrian pushes it back down.

"It's too hard. I should just give up already."

"You've given it up all your life." She didn't mean it to come out harsh.

"I know," Adrian says, not taking it harshly. "You know I want to learn."

Adrian huffs and flicks his fingers through the notecards. He lands on a bronzed, rectangular card. "What's this one?"

"Oh, that's the invitation to the Ball," Jazz says, cuddling up beside him.

Adrian's eyes enlarge. He taps under a word. "What the heck does that say?"

Jazz giggles. "Masquerade."

Adrian looks at her like she's not speaking English.

Jazz kisses his cheek, unable to handle how cute he looks. "It means masked. It's a Ball where everyone wears a mask. And formal wear, of course."

Adrian drops the invitation and shakes his head. "Why not just say Masked Ball then? Why do they have to make everything so difficult?"

Jazz rubs his back and feels the sweat through his shirt. "You'll get the hang of it. You're too smart not to."

Adrian smirks. "I don't know why you have so much faith in me." He looks her up and down and smiles. "We should hit the showers."

Jazz presses her lips against his, and her airy laugh filters through again. "I don't mind staying like this."

A whisper of a grumble tumbles out of Adrian as he pulls himself to standing. "I'm way too gross," he says, taking off his shirt.

Jazz gets up and moves close to him as he turns to toss his shirt. She doesn't mean to, but a gasp shoots from her lips. She's never gotten used to the scars that cross his back.

"You ok?" he asks, turning in concern.

Her fingertips touch the large scar across his torso, and he takes her hand and kisses it.

"Why won't you tell me what happened?" she whispers, a frown dragging down the corners of her mouth.

"It's all from a past that led me to you," he says, caressing the side of her face and then kissing her. He pulls out of the kiss, and says, "Now, seriously. I need a shower."

Jazz smiles and nods. Her smile is a facade. Her heart hurts that some horrible things happened to him in his childhood. She wants to take every single one of them back.

Adrian slings a towel over his shoulder, and it covers most of his back. Jazz leaves for the opposite end of the hall for the female bathroom.

When she enters the bathroom, Aria is at the mirror, brushing her damp hair. Her reflection smiles at Jazz.

"How was your run?"

"Good," Jazz says, her limp smile trying to prove real.

Aria lowers the brush and turns to Jazz. "What's wrong?"

Jazz shakes her head. "Nothing."

"Jazz?"

Jazz huffs, pulling her raven hair from its ponytail and shaking it out like it's a reset button.

"I'm worried about Adrian," she admits.

"Why? What happened?"

Jazz leans against the wall by Aria. "It's his past. He doesn't open up to me about it. I know the stuff with his parents, but everything from then to opening the shelter is a mystery. He has scars that tell a secret tale."

Aria pats Jazz's shoulder. "Give him time." She waggles her foot, covered by a moon boot from her own past hell. "Even when something is in the past, it can still feel present. And when you're out of that situation, you want nothing more than to forget the pain and soak up the happiness of being free."

Jazz pulls herself off the wall, feeling like a selfish brat. "You're right. I shouldn't expect more from him. We have already discussed so much. And I know that was painful for him. I shouldn't force him to tell me more. That's worst-girlfriend-of-the-year material."

"He loves you," Aria says, grinning. "If he talks about it with anyone, it will be you. When the time is right."

"How are things going with you and Eddy?" Jazz asks. "As far as I can tell, you two look better together every day."

"He's amazing. I don't understand how I got so lucky to have such an amazing man by my side."

"I'm so happy he has you. He now thinks about his own life and happiness. Not just concentrating on the rest of us."

"He has a way to go. He's still stressed out."

"It's hard to unwind when your brain is hardwired to work all the time."

"You'd know all about that, Miss Workaholic."

"Work is an addiction or a pastime. I love it either way." She laughs. "Not as much as I love Adrian, though."

Aria giggles. "Look at you go."

"I'm learning to put him first."

"Can I shadow you today?" Aria asks, returning to brushing

her hair. "I want to learn how to support people better."

"You know I'm always happy to have you with me," Jazz replies, "but I think you should start following Adrian. You and he have more in common and can interact with people on the same level. It's a skill I just don't have."

"Talking to people like we do isn't a skill," Aria says, giggling at their reflections.

"Oh, believe me, it is. I was raised to speak to people like I'm in a board meeting. Formality was everything when I was growing up. I'm having a tough time breaking it."

Aria gives her a wink. "You're doing fine."

"You should talk to Adrian about working with him."

Aria nods. "I will."

Risk

Caden watches his mother with disdain. She fawns over his father like he's a great king and she's his faithful servant.

It's not the subservient aspect that turns Caden off, it's the fact there's no challenge. His mother plays the role so effortlessly, his father never has to convince her of anything. His mother is always at his beck and call, ready to anticipate Bradford's needs.

Caden's mind wanders to his past interactions with Jazz Abadi. A strong-willed, confident, and independent woman. They grew up together, attending the same elite high school, and were supposed to be in the same graduating class at university. That was until the overachieving Jazz doubled her workload and graduated early.

Jazz has never fallen for his charm. He watched her relationship with Ethan Roth play out on social media. He saw the frustration and anger Ethan displayed when Jazz didn't follow along with his games.

Caden would have acted differently in that situation. Jazz makes him laugh. He loves the thrill of the chase. The strategy and game playing it takes to win over a woman like Jazz Abadi. It took no effort to get those girls on to his yacht. Every day, women throw themselves at him, willing to do whatever he asks.

His father would kill him if he tried playing with Jazz. Her father is too important, and Bradford Walsh can't risk anything jeopardising their business and personal relationships. He already got a lecture after word travelled about Jazz kicking him out of her pauper charity house. Caden has resigned himself that Jazz is off limits. But it doesn't stop him fantasising about her and looking for her qualities in another woman.

Imagine flipping an uptight, buzzkill, prude into a sexy, lingerie wearing, slave. Caden's smile grows as he reclines in his seat, letting his imagination run wild with scenarios.

"Hunny," his mother's words pull him out of his thoughts. "Your economics professor called to say your essay was a smash hit. I'm so proud of you. You do everything so well."

"Thanks Mum," Caden says, readjusting himself on his seat.

It's always the same with his mother. Absolute praise. When it's all you hear from birth, it's easy to predict.

"About time that man saw your potential," his father adds with a smug grin.

Caden blows a raspberry in his father's direction.

His father glares at him. "I beg your pardon?"

"Why am I at university?" Caden questions. "It obviously doesn't matter."

"Sweetie-pie, don't say that," his mother says, full of beans. "You are the star of the university."

"Jacqueline, dear," Bradford interrupts. "Will you give me a moment alone with Caden?"

"You boys and your secrets," his mother says with giggles, excusing herself from the table and leaving the dining room.

"Don't you think it's a little too easy to get rid of her?" Caden asks dryly.

"That's what you want in a wife," his father says, swirling his wine glass. "You can have your fun and your risk with mistresses and escorts, but your wife needs to be predictable. Quiet. By your side at all costs. She needs to be perfect for appearances."

"That sounds insufferably boring."

"You should look for someone long term," his father says. "The Masquerade Ball will be the perfect occasion. All of Maiden City's elite will be here. The prime female specimens will be on display."

"Doesn't get my motor running."

"That's not the purpose of your wife."

"*Ugh*. I don't want to think about marriage."

"You have to, Caden. You must think about graduating university, getting engaged to an upstanding woman, and moving into an executive position that will lead to a future in politics."

"*Pfft*. No, thank you."

"I need you to get your head on straight. I'm doing all of this for you."

"Everything you do is for yourself."

"And I need you to uphold the standard when I inevitably retire."

"I can see you as a floating head in a jar, ordering around the city for eternity."

His father bursts into laughter. "Well, if they have the technology, I'll put my hand up for the experiment."

"It'd be better than you trying to turn me into your clone."

"You are the most ungrateful person on the planet," Bradford chastises and takes a slurp of wine. "I make your life so easy. You have so much potential to rule this city. Yet you sit here in boredom."

"I'm not interested in politics like you and Grandfather."

"Your grandfather built a legacy for us. Our name is across streets, buildings, schools, and parks. How does that not enthuse you?"

"There's only one me. I don't need to be a part of some legacy."

"Well, tough. You're a part of this. There's no two ways about it." His father rises from his seat, and a servant haphazardly runs to pull back his chair. "Get with the program, Caden. Start with finding a suitable fiancé."

His father strides out of the room, two servants following behind.

Boring.

Caden slides down his seat, tapping at the mahogany wood of the dining table.

"Can I get you anything else, Sir?" Clements asks, taking Caden's dinner plate.

Caden looks up at Clements with an idea sparking inside him. "Where's that new lady cop?"

"I assume you mean Officer Jackson, Sir?"

"Yeah, the hot one."

"I believe she's on patrol in the north wing," Clements tells. "Did you want me to fetch her?"

Caden grins. "I think my wing needs extra security. Send her up to my suite, will you?"

"As you wish, Sir," Clements says with a nod. He hands the plate to a server and exits the dining room as instructed.

Caden clicks his fingers at a servant who hurries to his side.

"Prepare a bottle of our finest chilled champagne," Caden

orders. "Take it to my suite with two chilled glasses."

"Of course, Sir."

As the server darts away, Caden casually pulls himself up. He straightens his loose tie and moves out of the dining room.

He walks through the main living area and towards the great hall. He stops by the ballroom, where work has been underway for weeks on the upcoming annual Masquerade Ball.

A stuffy snoozefest like every other year.

Caden leans against the doorway, folding his arms as he gazes around the room.

I need to shake this party up.

He thinks back to his father's words. *Potential, fixed, risk.* Caden plays with the words to find a new meaning he can get behind. He thinks of his father, ruining his mood at the Cherry Stems.

How will he like it if I ruin his party?

Caden wants more than shaking up the Ball. He wants his own event. Something fun. Something entertaining and upping the risk level. He wants to see if he can actually get into trouble for something.

His gaze lowers to the floor. More importantly, to what is under the floor. An underutilised large basement with a high ceiling.

A perfect setting.

The ultimate place to hold an underground gambling event, the same night as the Masquerade Ball. Caden can't imagine his father's expression if he is caught, and that fact delights him to no end.

Caden rubs his hands together, smiling. *This is going to be fun.*

He walks the hall, towards the staircase leading to his suite.

But first, a different kind of fun. Maybe Hot Cop will want to help me out with this scheme. I bet she'd look sexy in a little bunny outfit behind a card table.

Entering his wing, he gets a glimpse of the officer. "Why, hello there."

"Mr Walsh," she replies with formality. "What can I do for you?"

"I like that you're so eager to serve."

"You know the motto: to serve and protect."

Caden moves to an end table where his requested champagne awaits.

"Don't let me keep you from your evening," the officer says. "Just let me know what you need, and I'll be on my way."

"You're not ruining anything," he says, pouring the glasses. He lifts a glass high. "This is for you."

"Mr Walsh, I'm on duty."

"I know. To serve, correct?"

The officer's eyes give a distinct roll as she looks off to the side. Her indifference to him gets him warmed up.

"You seem uninterested," Caden says with a smirk.

"I need to get back to my patrol station."

"You're with me. That will get you off the hook."

"I'd rather do my job."

"You can do your job in my bedroom," he says, gesturing to his bed, which is the size of two kings, surrounded by rich mahogany and filled with impossibly high thread count sheets.

Her hands fly up in defence. "Mr Walsh, I don't know what kind of game you are playing, but you can't play it with me." She moves towards the staircase. "I won't be disrespected."

"Officer, officer, you have me all wrong," Caden pleads, trying to keep the mocking out of his tone.

The officer huffs and turns around. "What's my name?"

"Huh?"

"My name. Officer what?"

Caden's eyebrows arch, wondering the significance of the question.

"Mr Walsh, I have to get back to work."

Caden smiles at the officer, excited by the similarities between her and Jazz.

"To be continued?" he offers, gesturing to the bubbling champagne on the antique furniture, surrounded by lit, robust candles and rare artefacts from around the world his mother's interior designer put together.

The officer deadpans him. "Only call on me for work-related issues. I am not one of your party girls."

And with that, Officer Hot Body leaves his wing.

Oh, I like her.

Turf

Cara crawls through the cramp, cobwebbed attic and climbs down the worn wooden ladder. Whoever lives in this dilapidated home made a racket this morning, but then they left the house in unnerving quiet. She spent the last two days camped in The Limits after providing new intel to the Neon gang members, and then having everything in tatters thank to two deranged sisters.

The Limits are the embodiment of every problem in Maiden City. Fear is thick in the air, circling the broken homes and feeding the defeated people. Welfare payments are a joke in this city. The people here are uneducated, jobless, and undernourished. But Cara feels safer in The Limits than in the Nightclub District.

Moving around the clubs, she is always vigilant of an attack. A mugging, a beating, or worse. In The Limits, people stick to their own. The small tent town is always quiet, surrounded by trash cans lit on fire. The boarded-up homes are only vacant after a heavy-handed domestic dispute, or when someone is hunting for food or booze. Cara enjoys the invisibility here. It's just not the place for her. She needs the clubs and the wealthy patrons to use to her advantage.

She ambles down an alley, kicking at the loose gravel, back to her hub. Her garbage hideout in the Nightclub District. Central for her work at night and an easy getaway when things get hairy. Nightfall approaches as she makes her way up the fire escape to bury cash in a fresh garbage bag. As she contemplates buying food and hoists a leg over the window ledge, something whacks into her.

She struggles to hold on to the window frame, blindsided by whatever came at her. As she fixes her glasses, she recognises the two horrid faces staring back at her.

"What the hell!" she yells, pulling herself inside.

The Tremaine sisters have made themselves a nest inside her hideout. Cara glances to the hatch and it is sealed shut.

They're too dumb to work out it exists.

"This our place now," Hannah says, puffing out her chest.

"I told you two to take a hike," Cara scolds. "First, I gave you money to get lost, and then I try to reason with you at the club. What are you not understanding? This is my turf."

"And I told you I'd rather just take what's yours," Hannah says, jabbing her finger against Cara's collarbone.

"Can't we all stay together," Greta says to her sister, her frame hunched and timid.

"No!" Hannah shouts. "We have claimed this. It's ours."

"Why don't you just go to the Youth Hostel?" Cara asks, frustrated. "They have beds to spare."

"We ain't paying for no bed," Hannah says. "We taking your lifestyle, and you can just deal with it."

"You're not me," Cara argues. "You don't move or act like me, and you'll never survive like me."

"No, you're the one who won't survive," Hannah threatens and barges Cara against the wall. She fishes inside her pockets and steals the wad of cash.

"Hey!" Cara shouts as she thrashes against the girl's grip.

Hannah pockets the cash and then goes for her glasses.

Cara spits in her face. "Don't touch those."

Hannah responds with her trademark aggression and gut punches Cara.

With an agonising grunt, Cara hunches forward, palms pressing into her stomach. Hannah follows through with two hits to Cara's head, and then stomps on her foot. The heavy boot protects Cara's foot, and she kicks Hannah in retaliation.

"Hannah, stop," Greta pleads.

"Aren't you supposed to help me?" Hannah replies.

Greta squeezes Cara's cheeks, and tells her, "I told you to work with us. But you had to walk away. This your fault."

Greta smacks Cara's face. Cara falls backwards and a jagged nail pierces her side. The sisters come at her with fists and kicks. Cara splutters coughs and tries to lift her arms to defend herself, but the attacks are swift.

The sisters pull Cara up and push her through the broken window.

Cara shrieks as she hits the rusted staircase. The sisters kick at her battered body, and she's forced to tumble down the stairs.

She hits the bottom stair and spits blood on the cracked cement. Her vision doubles and her limbs swell. Nothing feels broken, but she needs help. She doesn't want to pass out on the streets as night falls. She's cashless, so the hostel is out of the question. She's in no condition to work for a bed. Not to mention, she served up thirteen people to the Neons.

She stands, holding her stomach and hobbling against a limp

leg. Blood drips from her mouth, runs down her nose, and her forehead is tender.

Man, I'm gonna pass out.

She has no choice. It's the last place she expected to go, but she's compromised everywhere else. She must get there before the beating takes its toll on her and she's unconscious in the Nightclub District.

She drags herself through alleyways and back towards The Limits.

I just don't want him to see me.

If I could just stay there and avoid him.

I won't let him get hurt again.

As Cara breathes, it hurts. Every inch of her body aches. She needs to lie down. She needs to shut her eyes.

Maybe I can sneak into a bed, pull the covers over me, and creep out later. A few hours of sleep, that's all I need. Then I can get my place back.

She approaches the front entrance of the shelter. She doesn't love the idea of entering any building via the front, but the back alley always has a lot of activity. Hiding in the alcove of the adjacent building, she watches the front door. No one is visible from the outside, and through the dirty glass of the door, no one seems to be around the entrance on the inside.

Creeping forward, she pushes her hand out to open the door. *Creak.* Cara cringes as the door is unhelpfully loud. She pushes on the door, this time pressing her back against it, and slides into the building.

The foyer is empty, but voices sound from the halls. Cara stands against the wall, her chest rising and falling with painful breaths. She slams a hand on her chest and pulls herself off the wall. With a limp, she walks in the direction of the bedrooms.

Despite the heaviness of her boots, she's learnt to walk in them without producing a sound. She moves into the left-hand side of the hall and keeps her head down. Two people walk by. No one she recognises, and no one that recognises her.

Phew.

Ahead, she spies the T separating the male and female bedrooms.

"Hey, wait up. Are you all right?" a voice calls behind her.

Cara swallows sharply. Her head spins, and she pushes herself against the wall to brace for a fall.

The male belonging to the voice hurries behind her and catches her before she drops.

"I got you. You're ok."

Cara's skin crawls.

Dammit.

Sister

Adrian sits on the couch in the common room as Max flips channels on the TV. He anchors his elbow on the armrest and slides his head into his hand, watching two boys and a girl playing pool at the other end of the room. They are all new arrivals and he wants to ensure they feel safe and comfortable without hovering over them.

Heavy footsteps sound in the hall, and Adrian and Max look to the doorway when it sounds like someone running.

Eddy skids to a stop at the doorway, puffing for air.

Adrian stands. "Ed? What's wrong?"

Eddy beckons Adrian closer, his breathing settling. "Come with me."

Adrian walks to the hall. "What is it?"

"I... I..." Eddy stammers, shaking his head like he's trying to make sense of something. "I can't explain, you have to see for yourself."

Adrian follows Eddy up the hall and watches his body language shift nervously.

"You seem freaked."

Eddy looks over his shoulder. "Just brace yourself."

Adrian gulps from the uneasiness in Eddy's eyes.

Jazz and Gene walk out of the donations room. They wave to them but then notice the boys' expressions.

"What's wrong?" Jazz asks.

Eddy hurries to his office and opens the door. Adrian follows him in, with Jazz and Gene following behind.

As Eddy moves to his desk, Adrian's eyes pan the room and then the air is snatched from his lungs. The rough and tough exterior of a ghost lies on Eddy's couch.

He kneels by the couch and his voice shakes, "Cara?"

"She limped past my office," Eddy explains. "I didn't realise who she was at first."

Adrian tenderly strokes Cara's reddened face. Dark aviator sunglasses sit slanted across her eyes, and her breathing is shallow as she sleeps.

"Who is this?" Jazz whispers as she and Gene stand in the doorway. "Should I call for an ambulance?"

"Let's wait until she comes to," Eddy says. "I think she just needs rest."

Adrian smooths back her dirty blonde hair and looks over her body for any visible wounds.

What have you gotten yourself into, Cara?

Her body shivers and Adrian sees the outline of her open eyes through the dark shades.

"Hey," he whispers.

Confusion covers her face, and she utters some groggy sounds.

"Take it slow," Eddy says, standing behind Adrian. "Don't lift your head too quickly or force yourself to sit."

Cara's eyes open and close as she fights to stay conscious.

"It's ok," Adrian whispers, clutching her hand. "Your home. You don't need to worry."

Cara rubs her chapped, blood-stained lips and stares at him. "Adrian?"

He smiles. "Hi."

"I'm not here," she croaks, fighting to sit up.

"*Whoah, whoah, whoah,*" Eddy rushes, clasping her shoulder. "Not that fast. You need to lie down. Looks like you've been through hell."

Cara falls back, and her eyes close again.

Adrian exhales heavily. Realisation crashes over him as he watches his sister sleeping on the couch.

She's back?

She's home?

Where has she been? And she's hurt. Who hurt her?

"I need you to stay here," his last running thought blurting out of him.

Eddy squeezes Adrian's shoulder.

"Adrian?" Jazz whispers, moving beside him. "What's going on? Who is this?"

"She's my foster sister," Adrian says. "I haven't seen her in three years."

Apprehension sinks into Jazz's face. "Really?"

Adrian scrutinises Cara's face. "Although, I'm sure I saw her last week."

"You did," Gene says, planted in the doorway. "I recognised her too."

"You know her?" Eddy asks.

Gene nods. "She brought me here."

"She was sneaking in here?" Adrian questions, unable to take his eyes off his long-lost sister.

"I don't know," Eddy says. "She just looked in a bad way. She needs rest."

Jazz fidgets beside Adrian and sighs. "I know this is terrible timing, but we have to meet Lucas."

"Who?" Adrian asks.

"The tailor to measure you for your suit," Jazz explains.

"Now?" Adrian replies, wincing. He notices Cara's eyebrows raise over her dark glasses.

Jazz's jaw tenses and she rushes, "It'll only take five minutes."

"Only five?"

Her shoulders slump. "No, it could take up to an hour." When Adrian's mouth falls open, Jazz adds hastily, "But I'll hurry him. Please? It was the only time he had available, and he needs time to get the job completed."

Adrian's attention goes back to Cara. "But she…"

Eddy interrupts, "I'll wait with her. She needs to sleep. Give her some space, and I'll make sure she doesn't leave."

Adrian pats Cara's shoulder, and whispers, "Wait for me."

Gene steps into the room, giving Adrian and Jazz room to move into the hall.

A few steps down the hall, Adrian stops and leans against the wall to catch his breath.

Jazz stands close, giving his shoulder a gentle squeeze. "Are you ok?" she whispers.

"I can't believe it," he hushes. "She's back?"

"I'm so sorry to have pulled you out of there."

Adrian stands tall and pulls his arms around her. "No, don't be.

I think I needed a break to take it all in. To get my brain onboard with Cara actually being here."

"You've never told me about her," Jazz whispers, a sadness to her voice.

"I'm sorry. It was too difficult."

"Like a lot of things."

"C'mon, let's meet Lucas and then figure all of this out."

Rest

Cara's eyes flick open. Her throat raw with broken glass, her chest is on fire, and her limbs are like cement blocks.

"How are you doing?" Eddy asks, wiping a damp cloth across her forehead.

Cara frowns and jolts her head away. "Don't."

"Do you remember what happened?" he asks, moving the cloth away.

"Stop," she mumbles. She adjusts her bent glasses and squints at Eddy. "Long time no see."

"Likewise," he replies.

Judgement hasn't left his face in all these years. I could do without it, Bud.

She crosses her arms against her middle and looks from Eddy to the curly-haired teen boy. A weak smile plays at her lips.

I remember him too.

"Finally, I've learnt your name," the boy says, intensely staring at her.

Cara smirks. "You finally made it here, despite your crappy sense of direction."

"Thank you for getting Gene here," Eddy says.

"Why are you acting nice to me?" Cara questions, her eyes lazily falling shut.

"Get some rest," Eddy whispers. "You look like you need it."

With heavy eyes, Cara hasn't the energy to argue, and falls asleep.

"There's a new girl here?" a voice asks, stirring Cara awake.

Cara's eyes blink open, her shades darkening the room, and she listens to the female voice talking with Eddy.

"Yeah, she's just resting on the couch," he says.

Using her peripheral vision and the aid of her glasses, she spies on the red-haired girl who has a fragile, nervous energy. She looks at Cara and inhales like she hopes to turn air into confidence.

"I'll see if she's wants to talk when she wakes," the girl says.

"No, not her," Eddy blurts.

"Adrian always talks to new people. I want to do the same."

"She's not new. Adrian and I know her. Just leave her be."

"It'll be ok. I'll just be another friendly face. A female face. That could help."

"What about the kids in the common room? They're new. Talk to them instead."

"I have spoken to them, and I will again," she says. "And I'll introduce myself to the new girl later."

As their footsteps move into the hall, the girl asks, "What's her name?"

"Cara," Eddy tells.

Cara's fists clench. She doesn't want her name bouncing around the building.

I need to get out of here.

She listens, and Eddy seems to have moved onto the common room with the girl. She drags herself off the couch and pivots her weight between legs. Her stomach is tight from the punch and kicks thrown at her. Her layers of heavy clothing saved her from excess bruises. It'll just take time before standing upright feels normal.

Cara hobbles out of the room. She'd love to elevate her leg for a couple of hours to relieve the pain, and then she'd be able to work tonight. But being at the shelter feels like a mistake.

"Cara!"

His voice is instantly recognisable.

Adrian rushes towards her. "Sorry, I got back as soon as I could."

Cara hugs her stomach and leans against the wall. "I shouldn't be here."

"Don't say that." He reaches for her shoulder. "I'm glad you're here."

She shifts away from him. "I lost the place where I was living. I just needed to rest before getting it back."

"I'll show you to a bed," he offers.

Cara averts her eyes to the floor. She can't stand looking at his warm brown eyes and empathetic smile.

I don't deserve it.

"C'mon. You look like you were in a fight," Adrian says, gesturing to the hall. "Get some sleep, and then we'll talk."

Cara pulls herself off the wall, still unable to look at him. "Ok. Just an hour or two."

Intense

Adrian does a final check of the dining room and the common room, before retreating to his room. He left Cara in a bunk in the room Aria and Tessa share. It's so bizarre seeing her again. His brain feels like it's upside down.

"Adrian," Jazz calls as he turns his office doorknob.

He waits by the door for her to reach him.

"Are you ok?"

He sighs and enters the room. He paces the same spot a few times before plonking down on his bed.

"I dunno," he mutters, as his heart races. "I have about a million thoughts in my head."

"You were quiet when we were with Lucas," Jazz says, sitting beside him. She rubs his back and adds, "Which was understandable. It's just us now. Wanna talk about it? About her?"

Her?

My sister?

Who I haven't seen in years?

"Not just yet," he whispers.

Jazz pulls him close, and without prompting, Adrian rests his head on her shoulder.

"I haven't thought about her in so long," he admits.

"I never knew you had a sister."

"We met in my last group home."

"Has she lived at the shelter before?" Jazz hisses at herself. "Sorry, you don't have to answer that. I know you want to take some time."

Adrian pats her thigh, and a smile lifts his disposition. "It's ok," he says, wrapping her up in a hug. "You make me feel safe."

He kisses her and takes in the concern in her eyes.

"I'm just trying to get my thoughts to slow down," he says.

She nods. "That's ok." She holds him just as tight. "I'll wait for as long as you need."

"I want to be happy she's back."

"You can be."

"She could leave in an instant."

"Would she do that?"

"She did."

"You said it's been years since you last saw her?"

He nods, smelling the sweet scent in her hair. "She left three years ago. We'd been living here at the shelter for almost a year. One day she left and never came back."

Jazz jitters in his embrace. "She helped start this place?"

"Yeah. She's sleeping right now. She looked in bad shape. I'll bet she'll be out till midday tomorrow."

"Why haven't you ever mentioned her?"

Adrian doesn't answer.

Because it's too painful.

Jazz seems to understand him telepathically and rubs his back, letting the silence do all their talking.

Adrian lifts his head, so his lips sit below her earlobe. "I love you," he whispers, and then kisses her neck.

Her hands press into his back, below his shoulder blades, and a breathy moan seeps out of her. She kisses his shoulder and whispers back, "I love you, too."

It's not in Adrian's nature to be the one leaning on another. He wants to be done playing this role. He lifts Jazz onto his lap, and her thighs fall on either side of him.

Jazz places her hands on either side of his face, and their eyes lock in an intense moment. "You know you can tell me anything, right?"

He nods. "I know."

Jazz leans in and kisses his lips, long and slow. Adrian slips inside her shirt and runs them up her back. Jazz's hands run down his chest and play at the fabric of his shirt.

"Being with you is the only thing that makes sense," he says, kissing her collarbone.

Her hands paw at his hair and she sighs. "I just want to be with you too."

Their lips lock again, and there is a hungriness to their kiss. Adrian lifts Jazz's shirt up and over her head. Jazz's hands are quick under Adrian's shirt.

Adrian's lips tickle Jazz's bare shoulders. His teeth tease her bra strap as he flicks it against her skin. His hands massage her taut torso, and she pulls his shirt up.

Adrian grins as she pulls his t-shirt off. She presses her body against his and her hands run down his back. He notices how her fingers run over his scars, and he wonders if he can keep avoiding the subject if Cara sticks around.

As his hand run down her hair, he slides his head back to take in the delicate features of her face. "I feel so lucky to have you."

Rose highlights her olive cheeks. "We are in this together," she replies, smiling. "Anything and everything. I stand with you."

Adrian's gut quivers with guilt. "I just never expected her to come back."

Jazz frowns. "Your sister?"

"I mean, I waited years for her to come back. Eddy kept trying to reason with me to move on. But I couldn't."

She touches his cheek. "Of course not."

"She helped me get out of there."

"What do you mean?"

"She planned our escape and got me out of the group home."

"How did she—?"

"—Adrian?" Cara's voice sounds as Adrian's door swings open.

Jazz shrieks as she slips off Adrian's lap, clutching her chest.

"Oh," Cara says, staring at the shirtless pair. "I shouldn't have bothered coming in."

"Don't be like that," Adrian says as Jazz leans forward to collect her shirt. "Why aren't you in bed?"

"Your girlfriend is beautiful, Adrian," Cara says, zeroing in on Jazz's cleavage.

"Don't drool on her," Adrian mutters.

Jazz pivots her gaze between him and Cara, pressing her shirt over her chest.

"My name is Jazz," Jazz says, commanding the room as she stands and pulls her shirt over her head and down her body.

"I didn't realise I was walking in on some hanky-panky," Cara says dryly.

"Do you want me to show you to a bathroom?" Jazz asks Cara. "Or are you hungry?"

Cara's lip upturns as she sizes Jazz up. "No. I don't need your help."

"Cara, relax," Adrian says, stepping between the women.

"I was merely checking you were ok," Jazz says. "You look in dire need of rest."

The attitude is cascading off Cara as she stands with her arms crossed and a scowl twisting her lips. "I'm not dire needing anything."

Jazz turns to Adrian and whispers, "Perhaps I should leave you alone to talk to her."

"Good idea," Cara grumbles.

Adrian's chest deflates and he nods at Jazz. His frown sinks in as Jazz walks out and his surly sister glares at him behind dark sunglasses.

"Did you have to be that rude?" blurts out of him.

"Me?" Cara fumes. "I came to talk to you."

"I left you so you could get some sleep."

"As if I was gonna sleep." Cara huffs and turns to the door. "I'm outta here."

Adrian reaches for her. "Stop."

Cara flings him off. "Don't act like you want me around."

"Then tell me what you are doing back here?"

"It's not like I really had a choice."

"You know I've connected the dots over the past year and a half. All these kids who describe the same crazy girl who showed them the way here?"

Cara scoffs, taking off her glasses and shaking her head.

"You've never walked in with any of them," Adrian continues, pulling on a t-shirt "Why are you here now? Because you were beat up? I doubt it's been the first time in three years you've been in a fight."

"What does it matter?" Cara argues. "If you don't wanna talk to me, just let me leave."

"Why are you being so aggressive towards me?"

"I could ask you the same thing!"

Adrian flops back on his bed. "This is getting us nowhere."

Cara flops down beside him. "I don't want you mad at me."

Adrian watches her lips pout and sighs. "I'm not mad at you. I miss you."

She grins. "Really?"

He whacks her with a pillow. "*Duh.*"

Cara laughs and lies down on the bed. "You gotta know why I left."

"Why would I know? You never said."

She looks up at him and his heart stops for a beat, taking in the vibrant blue of her eyes.

"I'm protecting you by not being around you."

"Abandoning me isn't protecting me," he mutters.

"It's not like that and you know it."

Adrian gets up, shaking his head. "No, I don't." He gestures to the door. "Do you want to grab something to eat? I can make you something."

"Fine. But then I'm leaving."

"You need to stay. You're barely standing upright."

"I'm not staying overnight. I'm doing fine on my own."

"You need to rest."

"No, I don't."

"Just come with me and shut your yap for five minutes."

Cara laughs, following him out of the room with less of a limp than earlier. She stays silent, comfortable next to him, and Adrian's nostalgia transports him to four years ago.

Wrong

Jazz meanders through the hall, shaken by Cara's abrupt entry into Adrian's room. She's excited for Adrian to have her back. He's obviously missed her, but there's some past pain he's not outright telling her.

He said Cara was here when they set up this place, Jazz recalls. *That must mean Eddy knows what happened between them and why Cara left.*

Jazz circles back around the hall, towards Eddy's office. Jazz needs this situation rectified. What's happening in their lives right now is a big deal. They have the Mayor's Masquerade Ball to prepare for. It's the event where Adrian will officially meet her father as her boyfriend.

It's a massive freaking deal.

The one thing Jazz doesn't want to be is selfish. She doesn't want to rob Adrian of precious time with his sister, but she's also wary and sceptical of this girl she has never heard of before.

Why has Adrian never brought her up? Because it's too difficult?

She knocks on Eddy's door. She turns the knob and pushes the door open as he says, "Come in."

Inside, Eddy and Aria stand by his desk.

"Hi," Eddy says. "How are you finding Cara?"

Jazz flops on the couch. "Who is this girl?" it comes out much more frustrated than she meant. "Cara just barged in on me and Adrian. I left Adrian to have some alone time with her, but it was time for me and him, you know."

"Don't worry about her too much," Eddy says. "I doubt she'll be sticking around for long."

Jazz straightens her posture. "What makes you say that?"

"It's typical Cara. She'd come and go during the year I knew her."

"Adrian said she was here when you started the shelter?"

Eddy nods. "That's right."

"Why have I never heard about her?" Jazz asks.

"Yeah," Aria drags the word. She brushes Eddy's cheek. "You told me you and Adrian started this place together. You mentioned other kids, but no one as important as Adrian's sister."

Eddy sighs and rests his head against Aria's. "It was just easier," he whispers. "It was clear she wasn't coming back, and Adrian wasn't handling it. It was just easier to take her out of the conversation. Take her out of the memories."

Jazz scoffs. "That doesn't sound very healthy. If I did that, you'd preach at me to talk about the person more. Like when you wouldn't let it go about my mother."

"For one, I was just out of high school when I met Adrian and Cara," he begins. "And two, this is far different. You benefit from bringing your mother into your life." He rubs Aria's back. "But I wouldn't tell Aria to visit her sister. That would be beyond unhealthy. Adrian and Cara aren't exactly a healthy relationship."

Jazz's back tenses and her head whips to the door. Fear taking hold as she wonders who she left her boyfriend with.

"Don't get me wrong," Eddy adds hastily. "They are brilliant together. It's just... Cara can be unorthodox. She doesn't speak to people in the best manner, and uses the wrong means to get things accomplished. Adrian seems to be the only person who gets through to her. When they are together, they are golden. But she leaves without warning, and that's the part I don't like."

"Because you don't know where she is?" Jazz questions.

"No," Eddy says with a shake of his head. "Because of what it does to Adrian. I don't want to speak for him, but last time she left it took years for him to push past the hurt."

Jazz rubs her sore stomach and swallows hard. Her mind is a rush of Adrian and her heart beats with a strong urge to protect him.

"Keep your guard up around Cara," Eddy says. "She says one thing and is thinking two other things." Eddy kisses Aria's cheek. "Promise me you'll keep your distance from her. Do not trust her. Even something as simple as her age she can't keep straight. Her story is always flipping one-eighty."

"I'll keep an eye out," Aria says. "But I won't ignore her. I want to help her."

"Sweetie," Eddy whispers, his eyes rounding as they gaze into Aria's.

Jazz stands. "I'm going to find out what she wants. There's just one thing bothering me. Why did she leave after the shelter opened?"

Eddy shrugs. "There was a lot going on. It was surprising because she was instrumental in the decision making. It was supposed to be the three of us running this place. My father signed the building over to all of us, that's how confident I was we'd all stick together."

"Wait, what?" Jazz says, floored. "Cara's name is on the deed to the building?"

Eddy nods confirmation.

Jazz's blood boils. *Oh, hell no!* How can she make improvements to a building when a disappearing girl is a decision maker? *She can't leave until her name is removed.* Jazz makes a mental note to call her lawyer in the morning.

"I'm going to find Adrian," Jazz says, leaving the room.

I need him to open up to me before Cara sucks him in and spits him out again.

Brother

Cara leaves the dining room after a man pulled Adrian aside to speak in private. She scrutinises the people in the hall, her eyes forever focused on targets for the Neons. She hits her forehead three times, reminding herself she helps people escape here to avoid drugs and gangs.

Cara breathes heavily, closing her eyes and clasping her hands in front of her face. She focuses hard on pushing out the memories of Tremaine House. Ever since meeting those girls, flashes of her childhood have clawed their way back into her consciousness.

Why did I say that stupid thing Madam Tremaine always said? I never quote her... Or do I and I never noticed before? I've blocked her out for so long...

She concentrates on ridding the memory, gaining a moment's peace with a blackened mind. And then Pippa waltzes in. Her mind floods with kisses, neon, the shower, the bed, the badge, the anger.

Her eyes dart open with a mighty gasp. She carries herself to the common room and stands in the doorway. Everything in the room looks the same. An old couch, a TV, and kids mingling at the pool table.

A girl with a black pixie cut and silver nose ring moves away from the group playing pool. A boy follows her, and his image makes Cara's heartbeat accelerate.

She almost loses balance as Dean approaches. "What are you doing here?" she snaps.

"Huh?" he replies.

Cara blinks hard, and when her eyes adjust, she realises it's not Dean. He just looks a heck of a lot like him.

"Are you ok?" the girl beside him asks.

"I thought you were someone I know," Cara mutters, leaning on the doorframe.

"My name is Max, and this is Tessa. You just get here?" the boy asks.

"I'm leaving soon," Cara replies, lifting a hand. "You don't have to bother getting to know me."

"Who did I remind you of?" Max asks, stepping in close.

Cara flinches, hating the sight of his face. He's youthful and missing the skin-damaging effects of cigarettes, but he's too damn familiar.

Max gulps. "Dean?" he whispers.

"Why do you look so much like him?"

"You should stay here where it's safe," Max suggests. "You don't wanna go back out there and live under Dean's thumb."

"Is that what you did?" Cara asks.

"Dean's my brother," Max admits. "If I can get out of his shadow, you surely can."

Cara's eyebrows raise over her glasses. "Brother?"

Tessa pulls at Max's arm. "Let's get outta here."

"Nah-uh," Cara says, pinning Max back. "You could fix so many problems for me. Dean would leave me alone if I gave you to him."

"Take your hands off him!" Tessa wails.

"It wouldn't be enough," Max says in a steady voice.

"Get away from him," Tessa says, trying to pry Cara back.

"What's going on in here?" Jazz asks, racing through the hall.

Jazz launches at Cara and grabs her shoulder, locking her arm behind her back and slamming her against the wall.

"*Holy shit,*" Cara gasps. "Was that really necessary?"

"Did I really see you threatening these kids?" Jazz says, fuming. She nods to Max, and Tessa. "Guys, get out of here."

The pair fly down the hall, and Cara spies Adrian moving towards them.

"Jazz?" his voice wavers. "What's going on? Cara?"

Jazz lets go of Cara and turns to Adrian with regret in her eyes.

"She attacked me," Cara blurts.

Adrian takes Jazz's hand. "You can't walk in and immediately start trouble," he tells Cara.

Cara's jaw drops. "You're blaming me?"

"Jazz doesn't attack people," Adrian replies, "she defends."

"It's ok," Jazz interrupts. "I'm sure it was all a misunderstanding. I'm sorry, Cara."

"Don't let that name come out your mouth again," Cara threatens.

"*Cara,*" Adrian scolds.

"What?" Cara snaps.

Adrian huffs, and turns away. Tugging on Jazz hand, he says to Cara, "I need a minute away from you before I say something I'll regret."

In frustration, Cara stomps into the common room. She collapses on couch when her leg aggravates.

Dammit, I forgot about that stupid staircase fall.

She rubs her leg firmly, wincing as the pain dulls. A small amount of blood seeps under her shirt from where the nail stabbed her. It wasn't a deep cut, but she could do without the sting.

"Hey," the timid redhead from earlier says, approaching Cara.

If you say my name, I will punch your lights out.

"How you doing?" she asks. "We share a room now. My name is Aria, and I can help you out, if you need anything."

Cara sizes up the girl, and her eyes glue to the boot braced around her foot.

"What happened there?" Cara asks. She doesn't care about the answer, but it's distracts from discussing herself.

"It was from an accident that brought me here," she says, sitting down. "I don't mind talking about my past if it makes you comfortable talking about yours."

"Look, Princess, I'm not looking for any new friends," Cara says, standing. She shifts her weight to intimidate the girl. "I don't care if you are a counsellor or mediator here. I'm not interested."

Aria cowers beneath her, not expecting the verbal attack.

"Don't get in my business," Cara's voice rises with sharp aggression. "Get your *stupid* face away from me!"

Aria crosses her arms in front of her face for protection, and yells, "Valeria, Don't!"

Cara pulls back. "Huh?"

"Hey!" Eddy's voice booms behind her. "Back off, Cara."

Cara whips around to him. "Then don't send your lackey in here to save me."

"I didn't send anyone in to do anything. Aria is just trying to be nice and make you comfortable." He pulls Aria into his arms. "I told her the welcome would be a waste on you.”

Cara frowns. “As nice as you always were, Eddy.”

“It’s the only language you respond to.”

“What’s going on?” Adrian calls, racing into the room.

Cara smirks. “What, the cavalry riding in for her?”

“Just Cara making herself at home,” Eddy mutters. “Nothing’s changed.”

“*Eddy*,” Aria whispers. “It’s ok. It was my fault.”

Cara notices a slight shiver to Aria’s limbs.

Eddy cups Aria’s face and shakes his head. Without another word, Eddy walks her out of the room.

“Are you ok, Aria?” Adrian asks with concern.

“What about me?” Cara blurts, arms out wide.

“What about you?” Adrian replies, walking towards her.

“Why are you siding with them against me?” Cara fights back, her body temperature rising under her layers of clothing.

“I’m not siding with anyone,” Adrian says, his tone calmer than hers. “But I’m concerned about the people I love. They’re my family.”

“Family?” she questions. “Aren’t I your family?”

Adrian’s eyebrows raise. “Are you? I haven’t seen you in three years.”

“So, everything we went through is just forgotten, just like that?”

“Of course not. But you were gone a long time. I’ve been here and grown close with a lot more people.”

Cara’s fists curl as her brother stares at her like she’s a stranger.

“I’ve wanted to see you for so long, but it’s just like before,”

Adrian says. "You pull me between you and another person. I don't want to defend you all over again."

Cara's cuts and bruises feel doubled by his words. "You think that's what I want?"

Adrian sighs. "If you want to go, just go."

"Don't walk away from me," Cara orders.

"I don't want you gone, but there's so much hostility between us. I don't want it to get worse. Can you please stay and get some rest? Sleep on it, and we will talk in the morning."

"I don't sleep."

Adrian turns and walks away. "I can't keep going around in circles with you."

Cara pouts as her brother walks away.

How does he do that? He's the only person who leaves me regretting my choices.

Harmless

Gene walks past the dining room, and stops when he hears Eddy and Aria's rushed murmurings.

"Are you two ok?" he asks, moving into the room.

"We're ok," Eddy replies, kissing the top of Aria's head. "Just getting use to Cara being here."

"Is she staying?" Gene asks with caution.

"She should rest," Eddy replies.

Gene notices the way Aria holds onto Eddy. "Are you ok, Ari?"

Aria smiles weakly. "I'm ok. I just wasn't prepared for such a scary chick."

Gene's eyes widen. "She scared you?"

Eddy pulls Aria closer, wrapping his arms around her.

"She yelled at me and I got a flash of Valeria," Aria mutters. "But it's not a big deal."

Gene's jaw drops. "That's terrifying."

"Cara's not like Valeria," Eddy interjects. "There may be mental health issues involved, but they aren't the same. We aren't in physical danger."

"Cara may have helped me get here," Gene says, "but it doesn't take away from the fact she's psycho."

"*Gene*," Eddy whispers.

"We should let the crazy chick leave," Gene declares.

"*Ha!*" a voice mocks from behind Gene.

He turns and hunches at the sight of Cara. "Seriously, what are you still doing here?"

Cara smiles with glee. "I think I might stay. Purely because you want me gone."

"There's something seriously wrong with you," Gene accuses.

"Me?" Cara retorts, slamming a hand on her chest. "What kind of person carries a backpack with no food or money in it?"

"When I left home?" Gene asks defensively. "I wasn't prepared to live on the streets. I didn't plan to leave, it just happened."

"Exactly. That's why I got your ass out of there and brought you here."

"And it was good being away from you. Why the hell are you here, anyway?"

Eddy steps between them. "Can you two stop arguing?"

Aria slips past them and into the hall. With loyalty prevailing, Eddy follows her out.

"She doesn't wanna be my friend no more," Cara teases.

"You can take your glasses off," Gene states bluntly.

"Huh?" she replies.

"What's with the glasses?" Gene presses. "You're indoors at night and still wearing them."

"Piss off."

"Seriously, what are you afraid of?" Gene grills her.

"If you want to know the meaning of afraid, keep getting in my way," she threatens.

"You want Adrian to hear you talking like this?" Gene scorns.

"He said you're his sister, but it's easy to tell why he never talks about you."

Gene's blood runs cold as he realises he is alone with *psycho girl*. His mind whirs on how to get out of the room without her grabbing him.

"My brother needs to stop acting like I'm an invader. For goodness' sake, I'm the one that brought him here in the first place." She slides her glasses down and locks eyes with Gene. "And you, for that matter. You know, I noticed you earlier in Eddy's room and in the hall. The way you look at Adrian is interesting."

"Interesting how?"

"Interesting like you're in love with him."

Gene gasps and splutters a cough. "What? No! No way."

"What's with the longing stares?"

Gene raises a hand and winces. "Get outta my face."

He moves to the doorway, frustration getting the better of him, when Cara blurts out, "I'll be glad to tell him."

Gene spins around. "What?"

"Adrian," Cara drawls. "He's my brother, and I'd be more than happy to tell him about your feelings. You know he believes everything I tell him, right?"

Gene's heart drops to the pit of his stomach.

"And it's not a lie?" Cara's smile mocks him. "You love my brother? More than a friend?"

"Don't tell him," Gene says in a harsh whisper, walking back to Cara. "Our relationship is nothing like you're describing, but I don't want you saying anything to him."

Cara winks, turning to the hall. "Good night, Gus."

Gah! I hate her.

His chest rises and falls rapidly as he's left alone in the dining room.

How dare she make trouble between me and Adrian? A little imagination is harmless. She'd be telling him a lie.

Action

Cara listens for footsteps. The coast seems clear as she sneaks out of the bedroom and down the darkened hall. She passes another bedroom and hears the murmurings of a restless baby and a mother soothing it. She keeps moving, sure the busy mother won't notice a girl probably on route to the bathroom.

She had stayed staring at the mattress above her bunk for an hour, waiting for the lights to turn off and voices to stop. It placated Adrian to have her stay in a bed. It is easier to leave without him knowing.

He'll be better off without me around.

He knows it's true. He could barely look at me.

It'll be easier if he remembers me that way.

Cara moves down the hall and hears footsteps at the other end of the T. She stops to listen to their pace. She edges forward to see a shadowy, petite figure moving along the wall. He manoeuvres towards the front door, and Cara leaps out to catch him.

"*Arghh!*" Gene yelps.

Cara clasps her hand over his mouth and shushes him. "What are you doing out here?" she whispers.

Gene mumbles under her hand, shaking his head to rid her.

"I'll let you go," she whispers, "but you can't make a sound."

Gene's brow furrows. His mumblings get louder and quicker under her hand.

"*Dude*," she scolds.

He huffs and his shoulders droop in resolve.

"Ok," she says, and lifts her hands away.

Gene spins to run from her, but she grabs the back of his jean jacket.

"Where are you running to?" she asks, pulling him back by the collar.

"Away from you," he fights.

"You were leaving the building."

"Not anymore if you're gonna follow me."

"*Pfft*. I have better things to do with my time."

"Then let me go."

"Fine," Cara says, letting him go and watching him struggle for balance. "Tell me what's going on."

"Bite me."

"You weren't being stupid enough to go into the Nightclub District, were you?"

"Stay out of my business," Gene whispers harshly.

"What the hell are you doing?" Cara whispers, leaning over to meet his eyes. "I got you out of there so you didn't have to go through that."

"Don't act like you saved me."

"I'm not saying I saved you. I'm saying I brought you here for a reason. You're too pretty for the streets. They'll eat you alive."

"Don't act like you know me."

"What are you hoping to achieve? Are you looking for drugs?"

Gene scoffs. "No!"

"Then what?"

Gene turns away. "Forget it."

Cara spins him back. "Tell me. It's gotta be big if it's making you go ahead with such a stupid decision."

"I'm just looking for some action," Gene blurts.

Cara steps back. "Action? Like a fight?"

"No. A guy."

Cara's eyebrow lifts. "You want a hook-up?"

Gene groans in frustration.

"There's no one here for you?"

"No," Gene mutters. "I just thought I'd see what happens at the clubs."

"Take it from me, nothing good can come from it."

"I'm sick of being the one not in a couple."

"So, you wanna make out with a junkie?"

"They're not all junkies."

"How would you know?"

"It's not my first night out."

"You stupid munchkin."

"Stop acting like I'm some little kid."

"You are! You're barely a teenager."

"It's hard enough being the gay kid. I just want to be around people like me."

"Well, at least you got one gay friend."

"Huh?"

"Me."

"It's not the gay part tripping me out... it's the friend part. In what twisted way do you think we are friends?"

Cara rolls her eyes. "Can you just promise me you won't go there? It's not safe. The Neons are crawling the streets looking for kids like you to target."

"No. No, I can't promise."

"Why? What do you think you'll find out there?"

"It's a shot at finding someone who likes me."

"There's like a billion people under this roof who like you. I was here for two seconds and could see that."

"Whatever."

"Is this because of your crush on Adrian?"

"Shut up."

"You want to find someone so you'll stop thinking about him?"

"I only think about him because I don't have someone."

"So, you admit you have a crush on him?"

"Stop tormenting me. Don't think you know me. You have no idea."

"You'll go back to bed?"

"You'll go back to your garbage dump?" Gene asks rhetorically as he moves back up the hall towards the bedrooms.

Cara folds her arms, watching his shadowy figure disappear.

He's not going to sleep. He's gonna try it again. Dammit. I'm gonna have to keep watch to make sure he doesn't go out.

She puts off her plans of escaping and stands on night watch. Ensuring no one leaves the building to go into the part of the city she calls home.

Beaten

Cara can't let it go. Yes, she hasn't seen Adrian in years, but to see him side with others against her. To not pick her as his favourite. It is destroying her.

After arguing with Gene to convince him to stay in for the night, she stayed awake, reminiscing about her years living side by side with Adrian. She had tucked those memories in a nice corner of her brain, but seeing him so attached to others was like taking a mallet to every memory. In one night, the only good part of her brain was smashed to smithereens, and now she wants to glue every piece back together.

When my money is taken, and my hideout is taken, I'll be damned if my brother is taken away too.

Adrian appreciates empathy and charitable acts towards others. Cara huffs and throws back the sheets on the bed.

If that's the crap he wants. If that's what will get his attention. Then that's the crap I'm gonna do.

Cara pulls herself out of bed, the tenderness to her stomach and limbs mostly subsided. She looks to the end of the bedroom where Aria stands by a ratty dresser, looking through the scattering of belongings.

"You ok?" Tessa asks Aria.

"Um?" she replies, getting frantic. "I dunno. I've lost something."

"What did you lose?" Tessa asks, haphazardly looking around.

"My rosary beads. They were my grandmother's, and I'd just die if I lost them. Oh no, where are they?"

Tessa turns and glares at Cara. "Did you touch them?"

Cara leans against the bunk bed, folding her arms. "Touch what?"

"Don't accuse her," Aria reasons.

"I heard you was a thief," Tessa accuses, storming towards Cara.

"I don't know what you're talking about," Cara says, meeting Tessa face to face. "But I'm sure whatever you guys got, won't be of value on the streets."

"Then why did you come here to rob us?" Tessa's voice elevates.

"I didn't."

"Then why are you so aggressive with everyone?" Tessa asks viciously.

Cara groans and turns away from Tessa.

Tessa swings her back around. "Answer me!"

"Hey! Hey!" Aria yells, breaking up the pair. "It's ok, I'm sure they'll turn up." Aria swallows hard and her eyes flick to Cara. "Right?"

"I didn't steal your stupid beads," Cara grumbles and walks out the door.

Cara stomps into the hall, and even though her boots are heavy, she hears the pitter patter of hurried footsteps behind her.

"Cara, wait," Aria calls.

"What?" Cara sulks, stopping dead but avoiding eye contact.

"I'd like to help you, if I can," Aria says, stopping by her. "Even just to listen if you need someone to talk to."

"What are you, a social worker, or something?"

"Not yet, but it's what I'm pursuing."

Cara pulls Aria to the side and pushes her glasses atop her head. "Then let me give you some advice," Cara starts. "You need to toughen up."

Aria's shoulders droop and she frowns. "Toughen up?"

"Look at you," Cara says. "Anyone could eat you for breakfast. No one will take you seriously or give you the time of day until you gain some street smarts."

Aria lifts her fists above her chin. "I've been taking self-defence. I can take you on, if that's what you're getting at."

A belly laugh erupts from Cara and she slaps Aria's hands down. "Stop being ridiculous."

"*Hey*," Aria whines.

"You need to protect yourself from people like me," Cara tells. "You don't know what the real world is like."

"You can't imagine the horrors I've seen," Aria whispers in a darkly serious tone. "Don't for a second think that you know me."

Cara steps back, grinning. "Ok, ok. Kitty's got some fight in her."

Aria points to the brace on her foot. "I didn't get this at a tea party. If I can take down my sister, I certainly have no problem handling you."

"So, why don't you talk to people like this from the start?"

"What do you mean?"

"Let us with confidence draw near to the throne of grace," Cara quotes.

Aria smiles, astonished. "Hebrews 4:16. You read the bible?"

"It was beaten into me." Cara huffs. "All I'm saying is, if this badass side came out when we met, I wouldn't mess with you. But I met a mouse."

"Because I believe in treating people with kindness." Aria searches Cara's eyes as she quotes, "Whoever pursues righteousness and kindness will find life, righteousness, and honour."

"Proverbs 21:21."

"I don't want anyone to fear me. When I came here, I felt safe because everyone was nice to me. I won't rough people up."

"Adrian's girlfriend didn't get the memo," Cara says, rubbing the side of her face. "She sure didn't care about slamming me into a wall."

"She deals with threats," Aria says smugly.

"Whatever," Cara grumbles, and moves down the hall.

"You ok?" Aria asks, not following her.

"Yeah, thanks Annie."

"It's Aria."

"You sure?"

"Yes, *Cara*, I'm sure."

Cara waves behind her and keeps moving.

"Gus!" Cara calls out as Gene scurries from the opposite end of the hall.

He turns on his heels and hightails it away from her.

"Wait," she calls, jogging behind him. "I just wanna talk."

"Aren't you supposed to be leaving?" Gene says, hurrying his pace.

"I just wanna make amends before I go."

"Tough luck. I'm not talking to you."

"Gus, don't be like that."

Gene huffs. "You know my name is Gene. Stop being a bitch."

"I'm not."

"I don't care about what psychological trauma you're running from, just leave me out of it." He opens a door and looks back at her. "And for goodness' sake, leave Adrian out of it too. He deserves better than you."

Gene goes into the room and slams the door behind him.

Rude, Cara thinks to herself.

She turns into the bathroom and huffs as she looks around. *Just as I suspected.* She examines the bathroom's plumbing and all she can focus on are the leaks and cracks.

If I can't do any good with my words, I can do some good with my hands.

Sorting through a nearby cupboard for tools or parts, she asks a few passersby if they've seen any. When they look at her like an alien, she decides looking on her own will be easier.

She pats down her pockets, already knowing there's no cash to help her out.

I could stop by the hostel and take some tools and parts, she considers. *Julius won't question me.*

As she mulls it over, she rubs her jaw, figuring her rep here is already low. Leaving to get parts and then coming back to fix the physical issues at the shelter can't do any harm.

Thrive

Cara sees Eddy in the hall after she finishes work in the bathroom. She straightens her posture and tries approaching him like she did the others.

"Eddy," she says, trying for a jovial tone. "What's up?"

Eddy's eyes narrow as he grabs the door handle to his office. "What are you up to?"

"Why does everyone think I'm up to something when I try to talk to them?"

"Because your default is aggression. Anything else is cause for concern."

"Oh, that's real nice."

"I don't have time for your games."

"I just wanted to talk to you."

"If you're serious," Eddy says, opening his door, "you'll come in for a private chat."

"Like your therapy thing?" Cara says, her lip upturning.

"If you're not serious," Eddy says with a shrug, and walks into the room.

Cara grumbles and follows Eddy into the room. *If this gets me closer to Adrian, so be it.*

"Take a seat," Eddy says, plonking down on his desk chair.

Cara slides onto the arm of the couch and taps her fingers against her bent knee.

Eddy's eyes stay on her, and his demeanour softens. "Say what you need to say."

Ok, so his words aren't softer.

"Cara?"

"What do you want from me?"

"You called out to me."

"Don't act like you care."

Eddy sighs and gets off his chair. He moves around the desk and sits on top of it. "Cara, I want to care about you, but I never know what I'll get from you. You always have me raising my defences."

"You should know me."

"I would love to know you, but I don't think I do."

Cara smooths over her hair and looks to the scuffed vinyl floor. "It's better for everyone not knowing me."

"Adrian knows you," Eddy says, angling his head to gain her attention. "It hurt him when you left."

"That's exactly why I left."

"I'm not talking about the physical hurt he was going through," Eddy explains. "It's the emotional hurt he went through. He was a wreck after you left. I don't want to see my friend go through that again when you run off this time. He finally worked through it all and stopped looking behind every corner to see you coming home."

Cara's mouth drops, and she slides down to the seat of the couch. "He kept waiting for me?"

Eddy leans forward. "He loves you."

Cara rubs her heart. "I love him too. But that's why I left. I love him too much to hurt him."

"You should have said goodbye or given him some kind of explanation."

"I thought I was doing the right thing by leaving. I would have liked to stay with him, but I was a magnet for trouble. And trouble always took it out on him." Her eyes well. "I thought he'd be safer without me."

"He came here with you," Eddy says gently. "This is a home you discovered together, and you abandoned it. It took a toll on him."

"I should talk to him," Cara murmurs, biting a fingernail.

Eddy nods, sliding off the desk. "That sounds like a good idea. Talk from the heart."

"I don't know if I know how."

"Just be truthful."

Cara nods as she stands. "I can do that."

Eddy gives her an encouraging smile as she leaves the room. She takes a big breath in as she enters the hall.

A few paces into the hall, she stops and leans against the wall. She squeezes her eyes shut as they prick with hot tears.

I can't believe how badly my leaving affected Adrian. Her head sears with an ache. *He's always so bubbly and positive, I was sure he'd thrive without me.*

She sighs and dips her face into her hands. A powerful urge to run takes over her body. To not face him and see another ounce of hurt in his expression. He's the only person she's ever loved, and she can't bear to see him devastated.

She pauses and lifts her head.

Love.

The thought of hugging him lifts her spirits and makes her heart swell. She keeps moving towards his room.

Lie

Adrian leaves the kitchen after helping Hector put away supplies. He straightens some chairs in the dining room and then leaves to see who is in the common room.

Around the corner, he notices his office door ajar. As he gets closer, he spies a black boot slipping out the doorway.

"Cara?"

Cara's body leans out his doorway. "Hi."

"Are you waiting for me?"

"I was hoping you'd be in here. I thought I'd wait because I wasn't sure where you'd be... and I wanted to talk to you in private."

Adrian hugs his waist and approaches the door. "Ok, we can talk."

"Don't look so frightened," Cara says with a smirk.

Adrian stops in front of her, staring into her bright blue eyes, and tries to find the girl he used to know. "I just don't know where to begin," he whispers.

Cara bites her lip and clutches his forearm. "Well, I do. Come in?"

He nods and follows her into the room.

With the door closed, they sit on the edge of his fold-out bed.

Cara pats his knee and whispers, "I'm sorry."

Adrian scoops up her hand and cups it in both of his. His eyes stay on their hands, unable to meet her face or accept her apology. In his quiet, he recognises there's no anger spilling out of him.

"I thought I was doing the right thing," Cara continues.

Adrian laces his fingers between hers and squeezes her hand. "It never feels like the right thing being away from you."

Cara slides her head by his and sighs out. "I'm sorry. I just couldn't stand another second seeing you get hurt. When getting you out of that hellhole didn't stop it, I knew I was the problem. I was always going to be the problem."

"It wasn't your fault," Adrian says, frowning as he leans his head against hers.

"Don't lie," she says with a hint of laughter.

"I still didn't want you to go."

"You know why I couldn't say goodbye."

Adrian lets her hand go and pulls his head away from hers. "No."

"Adrian? Really?"

"No, I don't get it."

She touches his chin and swivels his face back to hers. "How can you think I could ever say goodbye to you?" Her eyes well. "I can never say goodbye to you."

Adrian's chest constricts, and he pulls her into his arms. Silence fills the space. Fear of her leaving stays in the back of his mind, but he wants to forget about it. For the time being, he wants to enjoy some time with his long-lost sister.

"Max said you're working with the Neons," Adrian says warily.

"He doesn't know what he's talking about."

"Are you mixed up with gangs?"

Cara shrugs. "Yes, I know members of the Neons. No, I'm not in a gang."

"Do you have anything to do with the Hoods?"

"No. I don't even know what they're deal is. They keep to themselves. I've never talked to one or know anyone who has."

"You gotta keep away from the gangs," Adrian warns. "Are you messing around with drugs?"

"*Pfft.* As if I'd take anything that would slow down my brain function." Cara shifts away from him, and asks, "What is all this stuff?"

Adrian pulls out of the hug to see Cara gazing at his desk, and the papers and books strewn across it.

"Oh, that," Adrian says shyly.

Cara stands up to inspect the desk. "I saw it while I was waiting for you, but I was too nervous to take much notice."

Adrian rubs the side of his forehead, wincing. "I'm learning to read."

"No way," Cara says with a grin, walking around the desk. "I never would have guessed you'd give it another go."

"Jazz persuaded me," Adrian says with a blush. "She's worth it. But I still suck."

Cara grabs a book and sits down on the desk chair. "C'mon, you got this. Stop getting in your head. You gotta take your time and sound out the letters."

"I keep mixing up the letters," he says, pushing away the page Cara shows him.

"You just need a memory trick to help you," Cara says, flicking through the book. "Like a rhyme or something. Don't you remember the one I taught you?"

"I couldn't get the hang of it back then. How come you could learn so easily?"

Cara scoffs. "I don't know if I'd call it easy. They beat me if I messed up my reading or spelling."

Adrian's stomach drops. "*Geez*. Yeah, sorry, I forgot."

Cara bats a hand. "Forget it. So, what's so special about this girl that she's got you pushing through the hell of reading?"

A goofy grin slips over Adrian's lips, and he leans back against his elbows. "Oh, you have no idea."

Interest consumes Cara. "Tell me more."

"She's so smart, and strong, and independent, and caring..."

"Wow, lovesick much?" Cara teases.

"I really love her."

Cara's expression drops from fun to serious. "Love?"

Adrian smiles. "Yeah."

"Oh. I didn't expect you to have gotten so serious with someone."

"We met a couple of months ago. I didn't date anyone before her."

Cara shuffles through more papers on the desk and picks up a card. "Why do you have an invitation to the Mayor's Ball?"

"It's Jazz's invitation."

"Huh? How did your girlfriend get invited to such a snooty, snob event?"

Adrian's jaw rocks as he tries to find the best way to explain his history with Jazz and her past.

"Adrian?"

"Jazz is rich."

"Come again?"

"She's Sovereign Hill rich."

Cara falls back on the desk chair. "If she's so rich, what the hell is she doing here?"

"It's complicated," Adrian says, getting up to pace the room. "She came here when she needed help. She was in line to take over her father's company, but she had an identity crisis. Long story short, she's here to help keep this place running. She's funding the shelter."

Cara laughs. "You're kidding. You're sleeping with her to get her money?"

Adrian stops pacing and glares at Cara with disgust. "Don't be foul. I'm not using Jazz."

"Don't get shitty with me. You totally made it sound like that."

"I did not. She wanted to leave her father's company and work somewhere where she can make a difference. And she is. I'm so grateful she's here and I wouldn't give her up for the world. If it's her or the money, I pick her every single time."

"Ok, ok," Cara says, raising her palms in truce. "I get it. You're in love, or whatever."

"I have to meet her dad at the Ball," Adrian says, lowering his tone as he picks up the invitation. "I want to make a good impression, but I know he won't approve of me. I'm not good enough for her."

"Shut up," Cara says, standing. "You're a courageous, caring, and selfless man. Frankly, I'm not so sure this girl is good enough for my brother."

Adrian smirks. "Trying the protective sibling thing, are you?"

"Well, if I must leave you with someone, I want to know they are the very best for you."

"But you're not," Adrian says, reaching out and taking her hand. "Right? You're not leaving again?"

She bites her lip and shrugs. "I'm sticking around as long as I can. What's this company her father owns?"

"It's a fitness chain. Ultimate ME."

Cara nods, eyes lifting to the right like she's making a mental note.

"Don't go interrogating her," Adrian says. "She's a good person. Be nice to her."

Cara smiles. "Always."

Hate

Cara's heart rate skyrockets. She leaves Adrian's room with a sweat gathering in her palms.

His girlfriend is rich? She lives in Sovereign Hill? She's the embodiment of everything we hate.

And he LOVES her? What?

How can he love another person? We were special. We found each other first. Now he loves her?

Jazz fills Cara's mind. *Gah! I hate her!*

...Pippa.

Cara scrunches her eyes closed, shaking her head vigorously.

Why did she pop into my head? Ugh!

She cracks her knuckles and marches down the hall. She uses time away from Adrian to let the new information set in. Her head is a jumble until one word calms her thoughts.

Rich.

Jazz is rich. Jazz could solve all her problems. Jazz could be one giant payday.

Cara walks past a half-opened door and spies racks of clothing. Walking between the racks is the curly mop of hair belonging to her little friend.

"Hey there," she says, pushing the door wide open.

Gene grizzles. "Why must you keep harassing me? I thought you were gonna be gone by now."

"Settle down, would ya?" Cara says, moving into the room. "I just wanted to ask you something."

"You've asked me enough questions. I can give you some new clothes, but that's it. Beat it."

"Beat it? Are you trying to get tough with me?"

"Isn't tough what you respond to?" Gene snaps. His postures droops and a small smile tweaks his lips. "That is, except for Adrian. Why is he allowed to be soft? Or is that just the good influence of not being around you?"

"What if being tough is from not being around him?"

Gene's smile grows genuine. "Good point."

"Anyway, he's here without me," Cara says, squatting to sit cross-legged on the floor. "And he's with Jazz. What's her deal?"

"What do you mean?"

"Well, she's some rich kid who's supposed to be running a big-time company. Why is she spending her time in this dump?"

"It's not a dump."

"You know what I mean. Compared to Sovereign Hill, it's a toxic waste dump."

"*Gee*, thanks."

"I'm just surprised Adrian let someone like that get close to him."

Gene laughs under his breath. "Jealous, are we?"

"*Ugh*, whatever."

"They are both great people who belong together. Leave them alone."

"You don't know what Adrian and I have been through. Your little run away from home stunt is nothing compared to our stories."

"I got beat up at home," Gene fights back. "It wasn't nothing."

"Did you get hit with a belt, a plank of wood, or an electrical cord?"

Gene mutters sounds, trying to answer.

"Did you get threatened with knives? Not be able to sleep because your body was so badly bruised?" She leans forward for emphasis. "Get branded with a hot iron?"

Gene gulps, his skin ghostly pale, and his eyes wide and round. "Th-that, that happened to you?"

Cara leans over, pulling down the back of her jacket collar to reveal the branding mark. "Look."

Gene creeps forward and leans over her. He hisses a gasp. "Who did that to you?"

"I was dumped at a church as a baby. Their forms of discipline were beatings," she says, straightening out her collar and sitting upright. "After I was too much trouble for the church, they sent me to a house that specialises in troubled girls. The brand came from my guardian who slapped me with her surname." She frowns at Gene. "I don't know what my real first name is, or if I even have one. A nun named me Cara." She sniggers at the thought. "It means beloved. Can you believe that?"

Gene drops to the floor with exhaustion. "That all happened to you?"

"I had no free will at Tremaine House. They were really strict on education and chores. I couldn't believe the punishments were harsher than what the nuns did." She clears her throat roughly. "I made sure I was so much trouble that Tremaine dumped me too. Then I found Adrian."

"I can see why you stuck with him after all of that. I'm sorry it happened to you."

"You were beaten because you are gay?" she asks.

Gene nods.

"Growing up, they would have beaten the gay out of me too," Cara says. "So, I didn't tell them. You're really brave to come out when you knew abuse was coming your way."

Gene winces. "Then what were your beatings for?"

"Not paying attention in class, cursing, sneaking out past curfew, fighting with other girls… Like I said, I'm trouble. But I didn't learn to stop when I got to the government home. I'd run my mouth and cause problems. But there they beat up guys more than girls."

"Adrian?"

"Adrian would never tell you what he's been through, and frankly, I shouldn't tell you my story either. But I'm willing to bet Miss Money didn't have it as tough."

"You don't know who she is?"

"No, why would I?"

Gene slips out his phone and opens to an app to show Cara. "Because she's Jazz Abadi. Her face is all over this city."

Cara takes the phone and scrolls through the photos. "Is this Collage?"

"Yeah. Do you have an account?"

Cara snorts. "No. I just hear people in the clubs and at the hostel talk about it." She keeps scrolling and clicking on images to see the location tags. "Wow, she shows everything."

"She's an influencer."

"She makes it way too easy to learn about her life."

"What are you trying to learn about her?"

"Her routine."

"Why do you sound like you're planning to rob her?"

Sick of his questions, Cara broadens her shoulders and looms over him. "Does it kill you to see Adrian and Jazz together?"

"Huh?" he squeaks.

"Do you wish you were her? So Adrian's hands would be on you?"

"What? No! No way. I helped get Adrian and Jazz together."

"But you're in love with Adrian. Surely you want him all to yourself?"

"Stop it," he snaps. "I don't want him. I love him, but I don't want him."

"Stop lying to yourself," Cara says, enjoying the teasing.

Gene snatches his phone from her. "Why are you such a mega bitch?"

"Thanks for the intel," Cara says, backing out of the room, "*Gus.*"

"I literally hate you," Gene mutters as Cara walks into the hall.

A commotion in the hall steals Cara's attention, and she follows people running towards the common room.

She moves into the room as people gather around the television. The bottom of the screen reads *Mayor Bradford Walsh Holds a Press Conference at Town Hall.*

The Mayor stands in front of a podium with microphones attached, gazing around what Cara presumes are a mass of reporters.

"Good afternoon everyone, and thank you for coming," Mayor Walsh says. "It gives me great pleasure to announce Maiden City's newest and most exciting endeavour. We are to commence work on revamping The Limits..."

A hush of whispers circles the common room as people shift uncomfortably.

"...Away with the dilapidated homes and crime-riddled buildings. We are giving the area a new name and will flatten the land to build industrial factories to create a new workforce. More jobs for the people of Maiden City. A stronger economy, and a brighter tomorrow."

The hushes become angry grumbles. The people in the room yell at each other, fists fly into the air, and feet stomp on the ground.

The bottom of the TV screen reads *Mayor Walsh Saves Maiden City*. Followed by *Our Greatest Leader Since The Late Vincent Walsh*, and *More Jobs For Residents Of Maiden City*.

The room fills with *boos* and people crowd the television. Eddy and Aria walk through the crowd, attempting to settle people down.

"Where are all those people supposed to live?" one person says.

"I know people back there. They can't afford to move into the city," another says.

"Hey, hey everyone," Max says, jumping onto the coffee table. "It's going to do us no good yelling at each other. We need to stand tall and work out how to save those homes."

"We can't take on the government," one man says. "They already created The Limits for us to live in. They control everything."

"We can't sit back and let this happen," Max says over the noise of the room.

Tessa clutches Cara's arm. "Do you know anyone who lives in The Limits?"

"Not directly," Cara says, biting her lip. "But I've spent enough time there to know the people."

"My family is there," Tessa mutters. "I don't want to see them, but I don't want them homeless."

Cara looks around the room, up at Max, and then down at her boots and groans.

Cara stands on the coffee table by Max. "I've found a home in The Limits many times. Yes, it's not safe most of the time. It's not healthy most of the time. But it's the only place we have."

She pans the room and lands on Adrian looking around at everyone else. Jazz hugs him as Adrian's concern pivots from person to person.

"Where are we to go if they take it from us?" Cara says to the crowd. "Do you girls want to turn tricks on street corners? Guys, do you want to sell drugs and get hooked on your supply? That's not a life. Let's stop this so-called saviour before he destroys us all."

The crowd cheers and agrees with Cara's words.

Jazz moves from Adrian and further into the crowd. "You all know my background, yes?" she says over the noise. "Mayor Walsh and my father are business associates and friends. I'll talk to him at the Masquerade Ball. I'll reason with him. I'll stop this from happening."

"We need more than words," Cara and Max say at once. They stop and stare at each other.

Tessa takes Cara's hand and helps her down. Max jumps down beside her, and the three move into a corner to talk.

"We need to talk this through," Tessa whispers.

"Trixie and Mo, right?" Cara says to them, keeping a straight face.

"It's Max and Tessa," Max corrects, unamused.

"Mayor Walsh needs to pay," Tessa continues in a whisper.

"I already have a job I'm working on," Cara mutters.

"A job?" Max says, sceptically.

"I need my attention on one heist at a time," Cara says, agitatedly.

"What are you planning?" Max says, getting in her face.

Cara shoves him back. "Miss Snooty Snob over there is getting what's coming to her."

"Are you pointing to Jazz?" Tessa says defensively. "Don't you dare touch Jazz."

"She's one of them," Cara argues.

"No," Tessa orders. "She's one of us. I won't let you hurt her."

"Don't take out your anger on Jazz," Max says firmly. He points to the TV. "Take it out on Walsh. Get him where it hurts. His money. His possessions."

Cara grits her teeth as she looks around the room. Adrian is too shaken to talk to the group, and Jazz walks him out of the room.

"You need to talk to Jazz about helping us and getting you a ball gown," Tessa whispers.

Cara splutters a laugh. "A what?"

"You need a dress to get into the Ball," Max says.

"Nah-uh. No way," Cara says, backing away. "You want me to rob the Mayor by dressing up as a rich snob?"

"You're the one who can apparently carry out a big heist on your own," Tessa fires back. "You gotta look the part and get into Walsh Mansion."

"If I'm going to Walsh Mansion, I'll find a way to break in."

"To the building with the most security in the entire city? I think not."

"I hear he has cops on his security team," Max adds.

Walsh Mansion. Filled with Maiden City's wealthiest people. That'd be a massive haul.

Cara groans. "*Fine.* I'll get the stupid dress."

"We can talk to Gene about altering the dress to hide pockets inside," Tessa suggests.

"I doubt he'll wanna help me," Cara admits.

"I'll talk to him," Max says. "I'll swing him round to help us."

Hope

Pippa watches him, and a fire grows inside her. The fire expands angrily as another girl awaits upstairs.

Caden Walsh is the epitome of what is wrong with this city.

Pippa is aware of the Mayor's infidelity and his patronage of call-girls. Most cops in Maiden City are. It's the number one rule not to report it. The Mayor is scum, who is helping to breed a new generation of vermin. Mostly young men who think it is ok to treat young women like possessions for their own amusement.

I won't stand for it.

Pippa returned to Maiden City and joined the police force because of her knowledge of corruption through the higher ranks and the prestigious upper-class. Since her patrol shifts of the Nightclub District, and witnessing the violations and assaults rampant in the area, she can't turn a blind eye.

It all needs to stop.

Her original plan was to keep records of who comes in and out of the Mansion to visit with Mayor Walsh, but her latest self-appointed assignment is Caden Walsh and his slew of *Caden's girls*.

That's what the girls call themselves. *"I'm Caden's girl."* It's the code for the guard to show them into Caden's suite. Despite the sheer volume of girls who have come by, they seem to believe they are in fact *Caden's girl.*

Pippa feels sick as she leaves the Mansion at the end of her shift. She desperately wants to break into his suite and get the newest girl out of there.

He is a disease-ridden cockroach.

She takes her patrol car into the Nightclub District. She parks in a lot behind a string of popular clubs. Close by is a cross street, Pippa noted back at the police station when searching for Cara.

Still in uniform with her gun holstered to her hip, Pippa exits the car and moves into the back alleys, scanning her surroundings. She looks for visual markers she recalls from the reports used to track down Cara's whereabouts. The sun is yet to set, and something tells her Cara is a night owl. Regardless, she retraces the steps she breadcrumbed across many reports.

There must be a clue somewhere.

Her hope climbs as Cara fills her thoughts. *Where are you, love?*

She edges around discarded garbage, careful not to inhale the rotten fumes. Aggressive and anxious voices squabble, stealing her attention. Pippa gazes up a fire escape and views two girls shoving each other outside a broken window. Surrounding them are empty snack food packets. Chocolate and grime smear their faces.

Pippa's fingertips skim her holster. "Excuse me," she calls. "Do we have a problem here?"

"Copper!" one girl screams.

They thunder down the stairs, wild hysteria in their eyes.

Pippa anchors her stance, readying herself for an attack. The girls reach the bottom of the stairs, and Pippa lifts her gun. "Maiden

City Police. Hold it right there."

"Dirty pig!" one girl screams and kicks Pippa's knee.

Pippa grunts, keeping herself upright. Her safety remains on her gun. Shooting civilians isn't why she signed up to the force, she just wants to calm them down.

The two girls' heads spin. Their faces are green. Pippa looks around at the empty packets of chocolates, pretzels, and cookies flying out of the open window above. It's like they had a wad of cash and blew it all on junk food. Their complexions have broken out, accentuating their large noses and angular faces.

Do they want to keep eating until they explode?

"Listen to me, please," Pippa says calmly, lowering her gun. "I'm holstering my weapon. I just want to make sure you two can be civil."

"We got help," the girl grizzles, swiping under her hooked nose and spitting on the cracked cement.

Charming.

"No one needs a cop's help," the others says. "I'd rather die."

"I won't shoot you," Pippa says, ignoring the girl's death wish. "Are there any other girls in this area?"

"What's it to you, Pig?"

"If you tell me I'll leave," Pippa negotiates.

"We already smashed Girl. No one else around here."

"You beat someone up?" Pippa questions.

The other girl leans forward, throwing a fist at Pippa. "Like we will you."

Pippa grabs the fist, throwing the girl's arm behind her back. "Assaulting an officer is an offence. You didn't connect, so I will let you go with a warning. Do you understand?"

The girl's companion shoves Pippa from the other side, knocking her over.

The girls shriek with laughter, running in haphazard lines into the nearest alley.

Pippa watches them and shakes her head. She stands, dusting off her uniform. While the area is quiet, she climbs the fire escape and surveys the area. It is familiar to the reports linking her to Cara's whereabouts.

Did those two girls rough Cara up to take this place?

The stench hits the back of Pippa's nostrils.

I hope Cara wasn't living here. It has disease written all over it.

Pippa decides on checking out Maiden City University Hospital in case Cara needed medical attention, the Youth Hostel if she took a bed, and then the shelter Mrs Williams informed her about. Perhaps she took refuge like the young Williams boy did.

I need to check on him, anyway. Walsh Mansion is trying to suck the life out of me, but I need to be strong and still do my job.

Trouble

Cara stomps out of the common room needing some space. It's one thing to mix with people on a dark dancefloor, but it's too much in daylight with all their eyes on her.

Is the Mayor seriously going to bulldoze The Limits? That's the safest place in the city. If I try to lay low any place else, the chance of getting caught grows sky high and I won't have a moment to think on my next move.

And what about all the people relying on The Limits as a place to live? Where do they go? Here? That's too much for Adrian to handle. He can't have that pressure thrown on him.

She remembers Adrian's reaction to the press conference. How his fear was about everyone living in The Limits. His worries are always about others far before himself.

I came here and started trouble purely to win his attention. Even when I knew I'd be leaving again. I wanted to alienate everyone close to him. Even though they'd be the ones staying close to him.

She wedges her back into a corner and hunches forward, closing her eyes. She blows out a breath.

Why can't I let anyone close?

Her mind shutters through images of her childhood. The

convent, the nuns, Tremaine House, Madam Tremaine, two foster homes, the group home, and then the shelter. All that abuse growing up still controls her, no matter how fast she runs. She came to the shelter and lived with others who promised safety, but she still ran.

The two sisters filter into her mind, and the buzzing in her veins simmers down. Her temperature falls from fiery to icy as she images of them pummelling her and stealing her hideout smash together in her mind.

What do I have to go back to?

They took what was mine.

Her hands press into her stomach and a sour taste lines her tongue. "I am trouble," she murmurs, staring at her heavy boots.

She pulls herself up, her head woozy with clashing thoughts, and moves in search of Eddy.

She bangs on his office door and shoves it open.

Inside, Eddy jumps from his chair in surprise. He slams a hand over his heart and exhales. "You right?"

"Sorry," she says, bustling into the room and collapsing on the couch. "I'm more messed up than just being rude, so you'll need to get over it."

"Seriously, Cara, you don't have to keep proving your rudeness," Eddy mutters, a hint of a smile appearing.

Cara rips off her glasses and stares into Eddy's green eyes. "I'm sorry." She taps at her heart. "This thing won't stop running and I'm having some kind of freak out."

Eddy steps around his desk, pushes the door closed and kneels in front of Cara. His eyes are purposeful and his expression soft.

"Are you having trouble breathing?" he asks with concern, checking her over.

Cara throws her hands up. "I'm breathing, but there's a freaking weight on my chest. I'm losing it."

Eddy takes her hands and pulls them down to the tops of her thighs. "Take it nice and slow. It sounds like a panic attack. Let's talk this out before the panic takes you over. What's happening inside your head? Is it the press conference, or something else that triggered this?"

Cara flings his hands away in frustration at herself. "A whole mess of stuff. These girls on the street, Adrian, Nuns, foster homes. Everything I tried to forget is in a tornado in my head."

Eddy steps back and sits on his desk. "Which is at the front? Let's nail one down and work through each separately. Adrian?"

Cara shakes her head as a wave of sickness rises inside her and threatens to erupt. Cara swallows hard and wipes the sweat from her forehead.

"I don't want to talk about any of it."

"You're a wreck, Cara. You need to purge. It doesn't have to be me you talk to, but it has to be someone."

"You know about this stuff, though, right?" Cara says with fear-soaked hope. She taps her head. "You can help make this better?"

"I can help you," he says with a smile and kind eyes. "You have to want help and want to help yourself."

"Isn't that the problem?" Cara says, standing and shaking out her limbs. "I'm selfish, Ed. All I've done is look out for number one." She groans and paces the length of the wall. "I don't deserve help when I don't help others."

"You don't?" Eddy asks, pivoting on the desk to watch her pace. "Didn't you help a bunch of kids find their way here?"

Cara rolls her eyes and her posture droops as she continues to pace. "That was barely help. I wanted them off the streets. I only found them because they were on my turf."

"And what brought you here this time?"

"A fight with two girls. We fought over turf in the Nightclub District. It's just like Adrian always said. I get into fights with everyone I cross."

"You fight with Gene, but I can tell you two care about each other."

She stops pacing and forces herself to meet Eddy's eyes. "It killed me when Adrian sided with other people against me. I wanted to turn him around and think of me as his favourite again. I didn't care about his relationships with other people, even though I wasn't planning on staying."

"Wasn't planning?" Eddy repeats. "Does that mean you are now considering it?"

Cara bites her lip, tilting her head sideways. "I couldn't. No one would want me to stay."

"You don't think Adrian would? Or I would?"

Cara snorts. "You? By the warm welcome you gave me, I think not."

"I was protecting Adrian, and then you threatened my girlfriend." Eddy clears his throat and then continues, "I didn't know your intentions, but I can see you've been trying. And your speech in the common room meant so much to everyone. You know what life is like on the streets. You're tough and smart enough to survive it. But most of the people under this roof wouldn't last. You know this because you bring them here. You still stand for the values that led us to create this place. You just have to believe in yourself again."

Cara takes herself back to the couch and sits. With a sigh, she says, "It's not that I don't believe. I remember everything from back then. It's just..."

She leaves the sentence hanging as her gut clenches. She frowns and pinches between her eyes.

"Take your time," he whispers.

"It's just so messed up," she whispers, her eyes welling with unwanted tears. She wipes them dry and sits back on the couch. "I was turning eighteen. They were gonna kick me out of the foster system. I didn't have to escape. I took Adrian and the other kids so I wouldn't be alone. How messed up is that?"

Eddy shakes his head, not following. "You helped them get out while you still could."

"I didn't want to be alone," she whispers, angry at herself. "Now all I am is alone."

Eddy's eyes narrow. "Cara... have you been punishing yourself?"

"I don't deserve people."

"How can you say that?"

"I'm trouble. I bring trouble. I hurt those closest to me."

"What happened to Adrian wasn't your fault."

"It kept happening. Even out of foster care it happened, and it was my fault."

"It's this city and what it does to people," Eddy says, leaning forward. "It happened here just a few months ago."

Cara sucks in a sharp breath, and for a moment her body

freezes.

He got hurt?

"If you don't want to be alone," Eddy says, reaching a hand out to her, "don't force yourself into isolation. You can stay here. Here is your home."

Cara doesn't take his hand, but he leaves it there, regardless.

Stress

Caden's grin hurts his cheeks as they wheel the roulette tables into the basement level of Walsh Mansion. He really took the underground gambling event to heart. He knows his crew will eat it up when it's held literally underground.

He has his own set of guards on his payroll. They do anything for a little extra cash. His father pays their regular amount, and then for the extra Caden supplies, they are willing to do anything he asks.

Puppets, Caden thinks.

His deliveries come through the back of the property, and his guards facilitate the move through the grounds and into the basement. The basement floor houses the wine cellar, kitchen stock, entertainment theatre, and bowling alley. Caden's gambling event is in an open space that was never fully renovated. His parents have forgotten the area exists, holding their events in the upper areas of the property.

Caden found the room a few months ago. He has held parties for the lads, where exotic dancers performed for them. But that was nothing compared to what he is now preparing. No frat house party, no back room of a strip club, and no casino will want to mess with him. His wallet is pulling the finest card dealers in Maiden City for the big night. Even the sexiest bar staff hired for the Masquerade Ball are poached to mingle downstairs with his guests. And a Neon member is dropping off a supply of party favours. Caden asked for the top shelf.

There isn't cause for concern in pulling this off. Caden has never felt stress before. His father's money has always financed his plans. Any trip he takes, any wild night out, any girl he dates. Everything comes from a never-ending money supply. A supply built by his grandfather, the late Vincent Walsh, former Mayor of Maiden City. Vincent grew up in Hamlet from humble beginnings and worked in many businesses. He came from the working-class, learnt everything about business, and grew an empire. Caden's economics professor raves about Vincent. How adored he is by the people of Maiden City, and how the Business District thrives because of the backing and development put in by this one great man.

Snoozefest.

Who cares what my grandfather did? It's all gravy now.

He looks over the grimly decorated room, smiling at what he presumes The Limits looks like. Not that he'd ever step foot in such a ghastly place.

What if there is no fallout from this event?

What if I get away with it?

If I do, maybe a future in politics wouldn't be so bad.

"Sir," an officer says, approaching Caden. "I just got word there's a lady waiting in your suite."

Caden rolls his eyes. "*Ugh*, another one. Can't they give me a challenge? This is too freaking easy. I need something more to get my motor running."

The police officer looks at him blankly.

Caden slings his hands in his trouser pockets and grins at the officer. "You want to take her for me?"

"Excuse me, Sir?" the officer says, choking in embarrassment.

Caden nods, his grin expanding. "Go on. Go upstairs and see what you can do to her."

"Sir, I..."

"Go on," Caden orders. "I don't have all day."

Bewildered, the police officer turns to move upstairs.

Caden throws his head back and laughs. *Ok, maybe I could get used to something in decision-making and law enforcement.*

Love

Adrian's hands cup Jazz's hips as she sits on his lap. Their intimacy becomes more natural by the day.

Jazz brushes back his hair and sighs. Her lips drag down into a frown.

"I can't believe what we saw on TV," Adrian whispers. "Will the Mayor really go through with it?"

"I heard him talk about this plan before I met you."

Adrian sighs, defeated.

"What happened in your past?" she whispers. "Back when Cara was here. I can see the hurt in your eyes. Her presence has made you relive things you're not telling me about."

As Jazz's eyes water, Adrian curls a finger under her chin and says, "Don't start, or I'll start crying."

Jazz lets out a weighted breath and collapses against him.

Adrian wraps his arms around her and strokes her back. "I met her in foster care, as you know. It was a big boarding house but still felt cramped. I felt alone until I met her, and she felt the same with me. You know how you can just feel lost until you find someone?"

"Yeah," she murmurs. She curls a finger around a lock of his hair. "With you."

Adrian holds her closer and soaks up her warmth.

"I told you about my parents and what they did to survive," Adrian says. "With them, I never felt like I had a family. Then I was bumped around in foster care, feeling the same way. Cara was like an anchor. We stuck by each other and it was less scary."

Jazz kisses his cheek softly like she has no energy to do or say anything else.

"My scars are from the group home."

Jazz wriggles in his arms, bracing for the rest of the story.

"There were loads of fights. Knives or things turned into knives. I must have been in the way a lot. I don't remember starting a fight, but I remember being at the end of some." He clears his throat and holds onto Jazz. "With Cara, what you see is what you get. She can't help saying what's on her mind. I liked her honesty, and with me, she slowed down. But with others... well, I wouldn't let anyone hurt her. I'd protect her."

"You got hurt when it was meant for her?"

"Yeah."

"She's the reason for all the cuts and all the scars?" Jazz says, pulling herself up as her voice raises.

Adrian brushes back her hair and soothes her. "Don't get mad at her."

"How can I not?" Jazz says, indignant.

Adrian puts his hands on either side of her face. "Because she saved me too."

Jazz's eyes grow wide as she takes him in.

"She got me out. She taught me to stand up for myself. She showed me I'm not alone."

"Then why did she leave?"

The question pulls the wind out of Adrian and he slumps against the wall near the bed. His hands run up and down Jazz's thighs as he readies himself to continue.

"I'm guessing because I got hurt again."

"Here?" Jazz questions. "At the shelter?"

Adrian nods. "Yeah. One guy who escaped the home with us, he wasn't right in the head. He'd say strange things or think he was someone else. He and Cara would constantly argue. I got between them, and he stabbed me under my ribs."

Adrian rubs the spot on his side as the memory hits like yesterday.

Jazz's hand presses firmly against his, and a tear stains her cheek. He wipes her face dry and kisses her lips.

Jazz runs her hands along his shoulders, up to his neck, and into his hair. Her lips press against his and their bodies magnetise.

"You know how strict and emotionless my childhood was," Jazz says breathlessly as she pauses their kiss. Her hands sit over his chest and lips inch closer to his. "Knowing more about yours makes me feel so much closer to you. I never want our bond to break."

"Me either," he's quick to reply. His hands slip down her low back. "If anything, I want to be even closer. I love you, and I want to tell you everything. It's just easier to forget it."

"I understand. I don't want to rush you to tell me anything. You know it's safe to talk to me."

"I know."

Their lips connect with electricity. Their passion flows through their bodies and their hands explore each other freely.

"I want to make love to you," Jazz says in their kiss.

Adrian kisses her harder, only stopping to say, "I want that too."

The door swings open.

Holding Jazz close, Adrian looks over his shoulder to see Cara standing in his doorway. He grumbles, "I need a lock for that door."

Jazz hides her head against the nape of his neck, her breathing hard and fast.

"I'm sorry, I'm sorry," Cara says, waving her hands furiously. "I want to make amends. Seriously. Sorry."

Adrian focuses on lowering his body temperature as this goddess of a woman sits on his lap.

"I appreciate that," Adrian says, trying for assertive, "but right now, get out and I'll find you later."

"Ok, later," Cara says, grabbing the door handle and pulling it towards her. "Sorry, Jazz."

Cara leaves, and Jazz slides off Adrian's lap, covering her face with her hands. Adrian notes the pink tones in her complexion and the mood dies.

Nimble

Jazz watches the apprehensive and angry faces of those who pass her in the hall. Her fingers flex at her sides as she plans a speech to talk sense into Mayor Walsh at the Masquerade Ball.

"Jazz," Cara calls out to her. "Wait up."

Discouragingly, Jazz stops for Cara to reach her.

"We gotta talk about this Ball," Cara blurts.

"Excuse me?"

"You gotta get me a ticket."

Jazz's face screws up as she comprehends the statement. "What are you talking about? I'm not getting you an invitation to the Mayor's Ball." Jazz relaxes her face, as she ponders aloud, "That is what you're talking about? Or are you asking me to get you a tennis ball, or something?"

Cara grizzles and nudges Jazz. "C'mon, you've seen Adrian."

Jazz's defences raise at the mention of her boyfriend. "What does he have to do with this?"

"He's a nervous wreck," Cara elaborates. "Imagine him round the Mayor? You know how irrational he can be. Do you really want him embarrassing you in front of all those fancy people?"

"Adrian doesn't embarrass me."

"I just mean… I'll keep him calm. I know how he can get. This is supposed to be about him meeting your dad, right?"

Jazz's jaw clenches and the ominous image of her father and her boyfriend clouds her mind. She has failed to hide from herself, her nerves about this upcoming meeting.

"It's not just about a ticket," Jazz says, shaking herself out of her thoughts. "You need a ball gown, jewels, hair and makeup. Do you expect me to wave a magic wand over your head and have all these things appear?"

Cara deadpans her. "You're rich, aren't you?"

Jazz scoffs. "You think I'll pay for everything for you?"

"You pay for everyone under this roof, don't you?"

Jazz groans and walks away from Cara.

"Hey! Where are you going?"

"I want you out of my face," Jazz says honestly.

Cara's heavy footsteps follow, and Jazz's head pounds with an ache of annoyance.

"What if he snaps in the middle of the dancefloor and makes a scene in front of everyone?"

"Do you think so little of your brother?"

"Do you not know about his hatred of the upper-class?"

Jazz huffs as she thinks back to when she and Adrian first met and when he discovered she is a wealthy heiress. He couldn't look at her, speak to her, and wanted her out of the shelter immediately.

Cara may have a point.

"How do I know you're not doing this just to drive a wedge between me and Adrian?"

"I meant it when I said I want to make amends."

"Why do you care if Adrian makes a scene at Walsh Mansion?

Wouldn't something like that be right up your alley? An upper-class event ruined by someone from the lower-class?"

Cara grabs Jazz's arm and spins her around, bringing them both to a halt. "I love my brother," Cara whispers. "I can tell he's too stressed to think about going to this Ball, but he'll do it for you. And wanting to be perfect for you is probably stressing him out more."

"You're trying to put all the blame on me?"

"He's the only person I've ever cared about more than myself. I'll look out for him. I promise. If he's fine, you two won't see me."

"Won't see you? Are you suggesting we don't tell Adrian about this?"

"Exactly. I'll stay out of sight," Cara says, letting go of Jazz and lifting her hands in a truce. "I won't ruin your night. I'll purely be there if a situation arises where I need to diffuse things."

"He's been without you for years. He has the coping skills to get through this without you."

"He has me now," Cara says forcefully. "Our bond is back. You know it."

"All right," Jazz blurts, taking a step back and flinging her hands in the air. "If you stick to the background and don't bother us, you can go."

Cara's grin springs from ear to ear.

"I'm doing this as an olive branch," Jazz says determinedly. "I get you into the Ball, and you leave my relationship with Adrian alone. No more interrupting us. No undermining me. You respect us. Agreed?"

Cara holds her hand out. "Agreed."

Reluctantly, Jazz shakes Cara's hand. "I must be out of my mind."

"You'll have a better time knowing I'm there as backup."

"I don't need my boyfriend handled. We are partners."

Jazz watches Cara's expression sour. Cara pushes for a smile and gives Jazz a wink as she walks away.

Good lord. What did I just agree to?

She pulls out her phone to contact her stylist to organise a new dress, mask, and jewels for Cara.

She lowers the phone and her stomach flips.

I can't keep this from Adrian. Lying or concealing information kills relationships. Especially when we are now closer than ever. I can't do that to the man I love.

After searching the common room, Jazz backtracks to the dining room and into the kitchen where she finds Adrian packing away dishes from the newly fixed dishwasher.

"It's so much easier to clean up in here since we fixed the dishwasher," Adrian says, moving a pile of plates. "Thank you for the millionth time for getting that done."

"It was my pleasure," Jazz says, approaching her boyfriend sheepishly. "It was only money I supplied. I don't get my hands dirty as Cara has done."

A breathy laugh seeps out of Adrian. "Something about Cara and working with her hands. It's the most Zen you'll ever see her."

"She's always been quick-fingered?"

"I guess. I think she likes seeing how things connect and work together." He gestures at the dishwasher. "Maybe if she was here before it got fixed, she could have figured it out."

Jazz shrugs. "Oh well, it's done now. I have to ask, how does working on some pipes connect with stealing from people?"

Adrian lifts another dish, his shoulders unmistakably tight. "What are you getting at?"

"She's nimble enough with her fingers to pick pockets. That's how she survives on the streets."

"And you think that's my fault because I taught her how to steal?"

"What?" Jazz gasp. "I wasn't saying... I wouldn't... Did you?"

Adrian meets her eyes, his face hard to read. "In a group home, you swap any skills that will help you get through your time there. I'd never been to school to learn anything worthwhile. I only had what my parents taught me."

"Was there no school at this home?"

"Not at mine. Cara came from a girl's home that had classes. She tried to teach me to read, but I still didn't learn well."

"The group home is government-owned, though?" Jazz says, not computing. "The government regulates school curriculums. How can they not deliver education to children?"

"Have you still not learnt how messed up the government is in Maiden City?"

Jazz exhales roughly, frustrated with everything she doesn't know about how the underprivileged are treated in the city she grew up in.

"And now look at what the Mayor wants to do," Adrian murmurs with an undercurrent of anger.

"I still can't believe Cara's speech in the common room. I didn't peg her for someone to speak up like that."

"There's so much pain with Cara," Adrian whispers, looking down as he dries a bowl. "But... there's so much good, too."

Jazz watches his eyes brighten as the word *good* lingers in the air.

"She helped me through a lot of stuff when I was younger," he tells. "We call each other brother and sister because of how instantly our trust and bond developed. I wouldn't be the person I am now without her. I'd still be scared and waiting for someone to use me."

"Use you?"

"That's what my parents did. They used me for whatever they could. Cara taught me to not let anyone do that. She's really strong." Adrian sighs and leans against the sink. "I don't want to lose her again. I need her around."

Jazz slides close and brushes his hair back. "You're strong on your own."

"I don't need her to be me," he explains. "I need her to feel complete."

"Even if she does things unconventionally?" Jazz asks tentatively. "Even if people get hurt?"

Adrian meets her eyes with sincerity. "She doesn't mean to hurt people."

Jazz swallows dryly and nods. "I understand."

He needs to believe in her again.

Adrian kisses her cheek, and then asks, "You wanted to tell me something?"

"Just that I'm going to find some common ground with Cara."

Adrian grins. "Really?"

"She's important to you. That means she's important to me."

Reunited

Gene pokes his fingers in his ears to drown out Max's words.

Tessa marches up to him and pries his hands back. "Just listen to him, Gene," she orders.

Gene yanks his hands away and huffs. "*Fine.* But I don't even know why you're working with this loon. She's not the most stable person under this roof."

"Who is?" Tessa argues.

Max lifts his hands to silence the two. "Look, arguing won't get us anywhere. I don't want to work with Cara either. She serves people up to my brother so he can deal to them and get them hooked. That's not cool. But she's just cocky enough to get revenge on the Mayor. She won't save The Limits, but it'll send a message. Then maybe more people will stand up. It's the only shot we've got."

Gene groans. "What do you expect me to do?"

"You need to alter her dress for the Masquerade Ball," Tessa explains. "Build in some pockets large enough for whatever loot she can steal."

Gene's face screws up with disgust. "You want me to help her ability to steal?" His mouth falls open as his eyes pivot between the pair. "What do you think Adrian would say about this?"

"You can't tell Adrian," they both say at once.

Gene stumbles backward from the impact of their words.

Tessa clutches Gene's wrists and stares at him with determination. "He can't know. Adrian is such a good person, and it would kill him to know what we are up to. He'd convince Cara not to go through with it."

"Maybe you all need Adrian to convince you out of this plan."

"Gene, this city is being destroyed," Max says. "We can't sit back. If they shut down The Limits, those people need somewhere to go. We all saw what this place was like when overrun." Max takes Tessa's hand from Gene's and squeezes it tight. "I can't lose this home. My brother wants me back in his gang, and I can't go back."

Gene's stomach flops and he grizzles his frustrations. "I can't sit back if it means that might happen. I'll do my part. But it's just the dress. Nothing else."

"What about her hair and makeup?" Tessa presses.

Gene deadpans her. His stomach sloshes again, and he nods against his better judgement. "Sure. I'll do it."

The pair thank him and bundle him in a group hug. Gene squirms away, telling them to stop thanking him. They laugh and leave him alone in the donations room.

He sighs out a slow breath. *This is crazy. Help Cara? Not tell Adrian? Stealing from the Mayor?*

His head spins and he sits down by a chest of drawers. He rubs his temples in anti-clockwise circles and tries a breathing exercise Eddy taught him to rid the stress surging inside him.

After a long while on the floor, Gene busies himself with folding clothes to distract from the ginormous task they have asked him to undertake. The doorknob turns with a squeak. He looks to the door and his jaw hits the floor.

"No way!" Gene gasps as Jazz walks into the room with a dress bag draped over her arms. "She actually talked you into helping her?"

Jazz lays the dress bag down on a chair with care. "I know I must be crazy."

"Nah-uh. She's the one who's full-crazy. When I heard she'd ask you for the dress, I thought for sure you'd laugh in her face."

"I very nearly did." Jazz sighs, frowning. "I don't want this girl at this event. But I have to think of Adrian."

"He can't want her ruining the night."

"He's reunited with his sister after years apart," Jazz hushes, her eyes mournful. "I've talked with Aria about how much I longed for a sister, and now I have her. I would fight anyone who tried to take her from me. There is so much family around me now." She drapes her arms around Gene's shoulders. "Like you, my precious one. We have to put ourselves in Adrian's shoes. Imagine if any of us were separated, how horrible it would feel. We must remember that. It's the only way to put up with her."

Gene hugs Jazz, hiding his face. "Why do you have to be the voice of reason?"

Jazz brushes his hair back and laughs. "I don't like it either."

They pull out of the hug, and Gene nods as he says, "You're right. Adrian brought us all together and would do anything for us. We can put up with her for him… Somehow."

Jazz smirks. "Somehow."

"Don't you feel bad we are doing this behind his back?" Gene's stomach is in knots. Tessa said Cara asked Jazz for the dress, but that Jazz didn't know about her real plans, just the phoney excuse to be there for Adrian.

"Adrian needs to see the good in Cara again," Jazz says. "He doesn't want to lose her. If something good can come from whatever she has planned. If she can really stand up and protect her brother, I want to help her. I want Adrian to have his sister back and feel complete."

"I don't want him hurt," Gene says, deflated. "Maybe he can know afterwards? Can we make Cara tell him?"

"That is if she comes back."

"What do you mean?"

"I have a feeling she will run."

"So, she's going to the Ball and doesn't want Adrian to know, and then she'll bail and not say goodbye to him?"

Jazz's eyes gleam with sadness. "It'll crush him if she leaves without saying goodbye."

"I'll be doing this crazy chick's makeup. I'll drill it into her she can't leave without saying goodbye. I don't care if it's hard for her. She can't be selfish again. Adrian deserves better."

Jazz smiles and brushes Gene's cheek with the back of her hand. "You're the sweetest, Gene. He's lucky to have you."

Gene's heart plunges. He catches her hand and pushes for a smile. "You have me too."

Steal

Gene's hands sling in the pockets of his ash denim jacket. His shoulders square and his back tall as he tries to appear older than his years. Since Cara's arrival at the shelter, a lot of conversations have revolved around the Nightclub District. Especially the back lanes and easy to access club rear doors.

After sneaking out of the shelter past midnight, Gene reminds himself to act cool and tries his luck with a club's back door. It's wedged tightly in the doorframe.

Locked.

Gene frowns and pulls again. With a creak and thump, the door pulls open.

Old, not locked. Nice.

Gene clears his throat and tiptoes through the darkened storage closet.

Seriously, why don't these places have locks?

Gene wades through the cleaning supplies and boxes of bottles, reaching a door which is framed by club lights. He places a hand on the door, feeling for the knob, and hears two voices on the other side.

Dammit.

Instantly, he plays out the moment he dies in his head.

Is that playing it cool, Gene? Stop panicking!

The voices muffle and flow into the rest of the club's voices.

Taking a few moments to compose himself, remembering Cara does this nightly, he turns the doorknob. Still imagining his demise, he pushes the door open.

He slides out of the storage room and into a hall. He's alone until a bar staff member passes him.

She nudges him and nods ahead. "Bathroom's that away. That's a storage closet."

"Ah, yeah, right. Sorry," he babbles, and hurries towards the crowd of people before she scrutinizes him.

The club is thumbing. The beat is loud, and the bodies bounce. Gene takes a quick breath in and out, swiping his hair back and remembering to stand tall.

Tall, Gene, tall. No looking scrawny tonight.

Realisation sets in that he's actually inside a club. With bravery, he looks around for any tall, dark, and handsome to look his way. He moves through the dancefloor to get to the booth seating. Everyone is a glow of purple and blue, cheering to the music and lifting their cocktails high.

Gene smiles at a colourful drink. *I want one.*

A set of hands pull at his hips. He turns around to see a gorgeous blonde man dancing beside him. Gene may stammer when he talks, but he doesn't miss a beat when he dances. Dancing will always make a better first impression than whatever mess comes out of his mouth.

Gene sways his hips and shimmies in a circle. When he turns in place, his dancing partner has moved on and is dancing with someone else.

Bummer.

He looks for anyone close by who might be interested, but he doesn't want desperation to show in his eyes. He keeps moving through the dancefloor, looking for the best spot to survey the area.

He stands to the side of the dancefloor and close to a booth where a bunch of university-aged guys sit, yelling over the music and laughing boisterously. Gene recognises Tyler Walker right away from Collage. Tyler is a typical rich-kid-jock-type. Not someone Gene would actively follow, but he dates women with flawless fashion senses who are always on the top of Gene's social media feed.

"I can't wait for the Ball," Tyler says, sinking into the booth and flinging his head back against the vinyl cover.

"I'm so over these stuffy tuxedo events," another guy responds.

"I'm not talking upstairs," Tyler replies. "I'm talking underground."

"So, it's real?" the guy across from Tyler, who Gene can't make out in the neon lighting, asks excitedly. "I thought Caden was yanking my chain."

"Underground gambling event," a voice calls over them.

Another face Gene recognises from Collage. Henry Gilbert.

"The hottest party of the year, cloaked in darkness, under the veil of the stuffiest party of the year," Henry adds.

"It's gonna be rad, bro," Tyler yells over the music. "We got VIP status, the hottest chicks who know how to work a pole, and the Neons are providing the sickest party favours."

"And it's going on the same time as the Masquerade Ball?" one guy asks, eyes bugging out. "That's insane. Caden really thinks he can pull that off?"

"If anyone can, it's Caden Walsh," Tyler boasts proudly.

Oh, lord. Cara might be good, but she can't pickpocket at the Ball when all that is going on. Will Adrian and Jazz have a good time if there's all this seedy stuff going on? Or is this what every upper-class event is like? All class on the surface and a crime spree on the bottom.

"I love your jacket," a girl says, pulling at the collar of Gene's jacket. "Where'd you get it?"

"Ah, it's vintage," Gene replies, shaken by her disruption to his thoughts. "I distressed it myself."

"Get out. Are you for real? I love it. Wanna sell it to me?"

Gene tugs on the jacket, smirking. "You'd pay money for this?"

"Yeah, darl. I'm loving it. Do you work in fashion, or just have a knack for this? Because your whole look is blazing."

"Ah, no. I'm still in high school. But it's the dream, one day."

"Are you on Collage? We should follow each other."

Gene looks at the girl properly for the first time. Her strawberry blonde curls, full pouty lips, and flawless, fair complexion. "Wait a minute, are you Rory Briar?"

Rory giggles. "Yep, that's me."

"You don't need a jacket from me. You've got to have a bunch of stylists fighting to dress you."

Rory hands him her phone. "Add your profile."

Gene searches his username and clicks *add*. "I'm Gene, by the way."

"How come I never see you around?" Rory asks, taking her phone back.

"I guess I study too much," Gene lies. "Are you going to the Masquerade Ball?"

"Yes, I'm all prepared. I'm going to steal the attention of Caden Walsh."

"You and every other girl." It flies out of his mouth before he can catch it.

Rory blushes. "I know, I know. So, are you here with anyone?"

"No. I was more looking for someone, if you catch my drift."

Rory wiggles her eyebrows, but her face doesn't respond. Botox already frozen her features. "I can introduce you to someone. Just so we are on the same page, men not women, right?"

"Hang on," Gene says, stars covering his eyes. "Rory Briar wants to set me up with someone?"

Rory tugs on his arm. "Rory is going to introduce you to someone who will buy you a drink. C'mon, Babe. You'll love him."

All Gene's blood runs to his head, and he's five second from fainting.

Ok, Gene. Get it together. This is what you came here for. Stay conscious.

Gene follows Rory towards the bar. He searches for who Rory is looking at, and a man stands from a bar stool. He turns towards them, and it's Ethan Roth.

Gene's stomach plummets to the floor. He stands frozen as the impeccably dressed man steps towards him.

Oh, lord. Not him. Anyone but him.

Ethan moves past Gene and towards a group of people standing near the dancefloor.

"Are you ok, sweetie-pie?" Rory asks, clasping Gene's hand. "You look like you saw a ghost."

Gene shakes his head, forcing a smile. "I'm ok."

"C'mon. Drake is over here."

"Drake?" Gene chokes. "Drake Malcolm? The twenty-year-old tech genius?"

Rory grins cheerily. "You know him?"

"Know of. I can't have a drink with him."

"Don't be afraid. He's super nice."

Rory pushes Gene to the bar. Before him, leaning against the bar, stands Drake Malcolm. Smooth electric blue hair, golden tanned skin, striking oval eyes, and chiselled features.

"Drakey, this is Gene," Rory calls over the music, tapping Drake's bicep.

Drake nods at Gene. "How you doing?"

"Good."

That's the best I've got?

"Buy him a drink," Rory orders.

"What will you have?" Drake asks, matter-of-factly.

"Ah, it's ok. Don't feel pressured or anything," Gene says, his lack of confidence crushing him from the inside out.

Drake smiles. "You look like a gin and tonic guy."

Having never tried alcohol before, Gene shrugs. "Sure."

Rory kisses Drake's cheek. "I'll see you later." She squeezes Gene's shoulder and says, "Good luck."

Without a moment for response, Rory disappears into the crowd.

Drake orders their drinks, and Gene awkwardly shuffles his weight between feet.

"You look tense," Drake says.

"Ah, a rough couple of days," Gene admits.

Drake takes their drinks from the bartender and hands one to Gene. "Then this is exactly what the doctor ordered."

"Thanks."

Gene takes a sip and lets the taste roll over his tongue.

Eww. It's gross. I hate it. Why is it so bitter? Or sour? Or... Ugh. This is gross. Why do people go crazy for this stuff? Ick!

Gene watches Drake's expression and realises his inner monologue is showing on his face. "Mmm, yum. Thank you," he covers.

Drake laughs, relaxing against the bar. "So, what do you do with yourself, Gene?"

"I'm a stylist." He says it so frankly he forgets he's lying.

"Nice. Rory wants a new stylist."

"We were just talking about that."

"You are cute. Why haven't I heard about you?"

Because I'm a teenage runaway nobody.

"To be honest, I'm still studying. Finding my groove."

Groove? Geez, he's two seconds from walking away from me.

"That makes sense. You do look young," Drake says, and takes another sip of his drink while he looks Gene up and down.

"You don't have to have a drink with me," Gene blurts. "It was Rory's idea. I didn't force her into introducing us."

Drake sets his drink down and places a finger under Gene's chin.

"Stop panicking" he whispers. Drake leans in and softly kisses Gene's lips.

Gene's lips tingle with electricity. His first kiss. His first kiss is in a nightclub. His first kiss is in a nightclub and it's with freaking Drake Malcolm! Fireworks disperse in his head.

Drake pulls away and a breathy laugh filters towards Gene's ear. "Have a good night, kid. You'll knock 'em dead when you're older."

Gene's mouth falls open as Drake walks away. Stars litter his line of sight, and his head is as light as a feather.

Ok, he knew I was underage, but he still thought I was cute.

Hands down, best night of my life.

Impress

Cara pulls herself out of bed the next morning, her back stiff with knots. She's not used to the spaciousness in the bedroom and the purity of the air. It frightens her. Every sound keeps her up at night. After years of being on alert, old habits die hard.

Tessa tiptoes to Cara's bunk. "We got you a car," she whispers.

"Huh?"

Tessa looks over her shoulder to Aria, who is at the other end of the room. "A while back Aria told me about how luxe Eddy's apartment is," she whispers. "How his parents are fake, rich snobs and have a phone service where they can get anything and everything with one call."

Tessa pauses as Aria walks toward the bedroom door.

"Good morning," Aria says with a cheery smile.

"Morning," they reply.

Aria leaves the room and Tessa continues, "Eddy can use this service. He also offered Max to stay at his place whenever he felt threatened by his brother or other gang members who try to lure him back."

Cara arches an eyebrow. "Max used Eddy?"

"Max went to Eddy's apartment last night." Tessa sighs. "To be fair, Max adores Eddy, and he needed to talk to him. He just may have overly elaborated on some things in order to get into Eddy's house… Long story short, we got the phone number and lined you up a car."

"And you're sure Eddy doesn't know? He won't keep a secret from Adrian."

"Aria said Eddy never uses it, and his parents don't keep track of the bill. They just use credit to pay for it."

Cara nods, grinning. "I remember Eddy's parents. It sounds like them."

"Wait, what? You know his parents?"

"Back when Eddy and I met. It's not important. They didn't like me, I didn't like them. But Eddy got them to give us this building, and that was the last time I saw them."

"It's so weird you helped start this place and no one ever mentions you. You must have really done a number on them."

"Shut up, would ya? Don't try to work out our situation."

Tessa moves away towards the door. "Wasn't gonna. Just remember I'm on your side. Ok?"

"Whatever."

Only your foolishness will judge you.

The sizzling pain of Madam Tremaine entering her mind torments her. She rubs the heel of her palm into her forehead and squeezes her eyes closed. With a large exhale, the agonising pain seeps away.

Cara pulls on her jacket and slips on her boots. She throws her hair into a loose ponytail and makes her way to the dining room. She has trained her stomach to not need food every day. Only when she has deprived herself for multiple days does it grumble. This morning she's interested in finding Adrian, not food.

She wanders around the tables and lands behind Adrian. "Hey."

He turns and his eyes are warm like the morning sun. "Morning. How'd you sleep?"

"Adequate," Cara replies, her answer for staring at the ceiling for six hours. "You?"

"Ok," he says with a shrug. "The Mayor's words won't get out of my head."

Cara pats his back. "Considering you're going to his house tonight, you might want to put it out of your mind."

Adrian frowns. "Bit hard to do."

She nods. "I know. Got any coffee?"

Adrian gestures to a scruffy guy coming out of the kitchen. "Hector's got some."

"Yo girl," Hector says jovially. "Need some java?"

"If it's black coffee, I'll take it," Cara replies.

"No milk?" Hector asks. "Sugar?"

"Just black," Cara says, taking a cup. "Milk spoils too quickly. When a bathroom is hard to come by, you can't risk it."

Hector's face greens with regret at asking the question.

Adrian nudges her. "Grab a plate and sit with me."

"Coffee is enough."

"You gotta eat something," Adrian urges. His smile brightens, and he teases, "I'm not sitting with you if you don't eat."

Cara smiles involuntarily. "Ok, fine. I'll take some freaking bread."

Adrian waits for her to collect a plate of food and then shows her to an empty table.

"Do you ever want to get away from this place?" Cara asks. "Do you ever want something more? Or are you happy?"

"I'm happy," Adrian answers. "No one else will help these kids. They'd be sent to a group home like what we escaped from. I'd be miserable if I left."

Cara chews her lip. "You're looking at me like you're trying to figure out how I could leave."

"No," Adrian says, shifting in his chair. "Well, yeah, but that was a different time. We were just starting then. I've seen a lot more since."

"So have I," Cara murmurs.

Adrian leans in, his eyes filled with sadness. "Why do you do it? Why do you live out there? This is your home. You put yourself through hell out there."

"It's where I belong."

"Bull."

Cara huffs and turns away from him. Her eyes wander the room as her arms fold over each other. Her eyes meet Jazz, who stares at her with intensity.

Cara smirks. "Looks like the girlfriend is jealous you're sitting with me and not her."

Adrian looks to where Cara is staring. He laughs, cupping a hand around his mouth. "I'm surprised you don't have two holes burning through you."

"Huh?" Cara asks, dusting her jacket.

"She's not looking at me. She's glued to you," Adrian says, his smile creating a dimple in his left cheek. "What did you say to her?"

"You're blaming me for her staring?"

"Maybe you said nothing, but you did something," Adrian

pushes. "More than just walking in on us."

"I'm not hanging out with your girlfriend without you," Cara scowls. "I'm not into talking about fashion and the best way to pose for a photo."

"Don't be so harsh."

"Then get off my back," Cara argues.

Adrian stares at her for a moment in silence, then looks down to his plate and eats.

Cara stares at him, biting into her lip as sweat builds in her palms.

She exhales loudly and blurts, "I'm sorry, ok."

Adrian looks up at her, the surprise rounding his eyes.

Cara smiles at his expression and laughs. "I didn't realise how much I missed you."

"I'm that forgettable?" he asks with a cheeky grin.

"You were incredibly hard to forget," she whispers. "It took a lot of work. I wasn't about to undo all that hard work."

"So, why come back?"

Cara rubs the back of her neck. Her hand slips, and she runs over the mark, permanently scarring her skin. She drops her hand and frowns.

"I was drawn back," she admits.

Adrian reaches across the table and scoops her hand in his. "I'm glad you stayed and didn't run off again. Jazz and I are going out tonight. Will you still be here when we get back?"

Guilt flips her stomach.

"About that," she pivots the conversation. "What's your plan for tonight? Have you memorised the perfect thing to say to Jazz's dad?"

Adrian lets her hand go. He sighs and sinks in his chair. "I'm way too nervous to think about it."

"Has Eddy helped you?"

"I've only talked to Jazz about it. I think she's freaked too."

"Do you remember what we did to act tough at the group home?"

Adrian's eyebrow arches. "You want me to act aggressively with Jazz's father?"

Cara *tsks*. "Did I say aggressive? No. Remember when we didn't want to be messed with? Stand tall, short answers, minimal eye contact."

Adrian smiles. "You mean how you taught me not to be a dweeb?"

"I just wanted you to stand up for yourself. A rich guy is a new type of bully."

"I see what you're saying. I shouldn't act scared."

Cara nods. "No nerves."

"I'll have to remember that when I get to the Ball."

Cara fakes a laugh and says, "Maybe I should go to the Ball so I can whisper a pep talk in your ear."

"Ah, yeah, no," Adrian drawls. "That wouldn't go well."

"Why? Am I not Ball material?"

Adrian cringes. "No. But you know that."

Cara scratches her head, feeling for her glasses she left in the bedroom. "Yeah, I know. I was trying to be funny."

"It was more weird than funny."

I guess I won't tell you I'm going, then.

"Whatever." Cara huffs and takes a sip of coffee. "How's the reading going?"

"With everything else going on, I haven't thought about it. I can't get the Mayor's press conference out of my head."

"Don't keep thinking about that," Cara urges, needing to distract him. "Why don't we go to your room and I'll help you learn something to impress your girlfriend."

Adrian laughs. "Why does that sound not so innocent?"

Cara rolls her eyes, getting up from her seat. "Just come with me, would ya."

Dangerous

Gene makes his way from the bathroom to the common room to meet up with Adrian before he leaves for the Masquerade Ball. He hurries his way past the front door, but a figure catches his eye, coming through the doorway.

Turning back, he is stunned to see a police officer entering the building.

The officer shows her badge and nods to Gene. "Excuse me, could I talk to you for a moment?"

Gene stammers, "Ah, me?"

I'm a goner. Someone saw me out last night and reported it to the police. She'll arrest me for being in a club as a minor. We practically live in The Limits here. She'll love locking someone like me up and throwing away the key.

"My name is Officer Jackson, and I'm trying to track someone down."

"*Whoah!*" Gene blurts, throwing his arms out wide. "Oh, no, you don't. Everyone under this roof is safe. You can't accuse anyone here of breaking the law or——"

"——Hey, hey," Officer Jackson says soothingly. "I'm not here to interrogate or arrest anyone. I'm just looking for someone to check they are ok. Honestly, I'm not sure if they are here or not."

"Gene?" Jazz's voice calls with concern.

Gene turns, relieved, as her heels click with hurry to meet them.

"Everything ok?" Jazz asks, placing her hand on Gene's back.

"Oh, Miss Abadi," the officer says, extending her hand to Jazz.

"Yes," Jazz says, trying to place the face. "Sorry, have we met?"

"No," Officer Jackson says as they shake hands. "I know your profile. Comes with the territory."

Jazz nods with a polite smile. "Of course. So, what can we do for you, Officer?"

"I'm Officer Pippa Jackson," she introduces herself, and then she double-takes at Gene. "Your name is Gene?"

Gene points to his chest. "Me? Yeah. Why?"

"Your parents miss you," she says matter-of-factly.

"My parents?" Gene splutters.

"Wait, are you sure you've spoken to them?" Jazz asks protectively.

A lump balls in Gene's throat. "Dad's hitting her again?"

Pippa's eyes grow empathetic as she gently says, "Your mother misses you very much."

But she helped him throw me out... He's too stunned to say it aloud.

Jazz squeezes his shoulder, and says to the officer, "Is this why you've come here?"

"Uh, no," Pippa replies, taking a step back. "I mean, yes, but I'm also looking for another person. A woman in her early twenties. Dark blonde hair, wears bulky clothing, and often seen wearing dark sunglasses to disguise her face."

Jazz's hands flex by her side. "And you think this person is here?"

"Is there someone here matching that description?" Pippa asks optimistically.

"Not that I've seen," Gene blurts. He grasps Jazz's hand. "Right? We meet everyone that arrives. No one like that is here."

"Right," Jazz says, following Gene's lead. With hesitation, she asks, "Is this girl dangerous?"

"No," Pippa is quick to respond. "Not at all. I just need to speak with her." Her phone rings and she pulls it from her trouser pocket. "Excuse me."

As Pippa moves away to take the call, Gene whispers frantically, "We can't tell her. She's a cop."

Jazz murmurs under her breath. "I know."

"This chick is nothing but trouble," Gene mutters, angry again at Cara. "Bringing the cops here."

"Six months ago, I would have told a police officer anything they wanted to know," Jazz whispers solemnly. "I had no reason to question law enforcement. But now with everything I've seen and heard… No badge or title will make me trust anyone."

"We've got to get this cop out of here before she sees anyone else she wants to nail down."

Pippa ends the call and moves back over to them.

"Do you have a card, Officer Jackson?" Jazz offers. "I'll call if this person shows up."

"Thank you," Pippa says, handing over her information. "I appreciate that."

"Of course," Jazz says with obligatory politeness.

"Thank you for your cooperation," the officer says, nodding to each of them. "And I presume I'll see you tonight, Miss Abadi?"

"I beg your pardon?"

"At the Masquerade Ball."

"Oh?"

Pippa smiles. "I'm working security."

"I see."

The officer smiles at Gene, and asks, "Is there a message you'd like me to relay to your parents?"

Gene cringes. "Ah, no thank you."

"You can call the number on the card if you change your mind."

Officer Jackson leaves as Gene and Jazz exchange looks.

"That confirms it," Gene says bluntly. "Thank the lord we didn't say anything. She's obviously crooked. She's on the Mayor's payroll."

Jazz drops her face into her hands. "What is Cara up to? Why is the Mayor already looking for her?"

Gene's insides quiver with guilt. "You think she has an ulterior motive?"

Jazz's eyes move like she is trying to calculate something. "What else is Cara hiding? I need to talk to Adrian."

"Adrian's already dealing with a lot. We shouldn't add on extra stress of telling him there was a cop here, and that cop was after Cara."

Jazz's eyes widen and her fingers snap. "Eddy. I'll ask Eddy."

"Wait," Gene calls as Jazz paces down the hall. "Jazz, wait. You don't wanna bother Eddy with this."

Jazz pounds on Eddy's door and turns the doorknob as Eddy is mid response. Gene peers around Jazz as the door open, and sees

Eddy by his desk with his arms wrapped around Aria.

Gene grabs Jazz's arm to yank her back. "See, we're interrupting them."

His heart pounds as fear of them discovering Cara's secret plans and revealing Gene's involvement writhes inside him.

"It's ok," Eddy says as he unravels his arms and strokes Aria's back. "We were just mid pep talk."

Jazz moves into the room and her energy decreases. "Pep talk?"

Aria bats a hand, an embarrassed blush to her face. "It's nothing. I was just worried about tonight, that's all."

"It's not nothing," Eddy says, placing his hand under Aria's chin. "Remember, talking out your feelings is a good thing. No more bottling it up."

Aria smiles as Eddy removes his hand, and she nods.

"This is about Adrian and me not being here tonight?" Jazz asks, guilt changing her demeanour.

"I want you guys to have a good time," Aria rushes. "Don't think I don't want you to go. It's just a huge responsibility looking after this place and everyone living here."

"Eddy is staying," Jazz replies.

"She always has my help," Eddy says, sitting on his desk.

"But he's got a list of people to talk to tonight," Aria says, settling back into nervousness.

Jazz places her hands on Aria's shoulders. "You'll be fine, Aria. And you're not alone. Hector and Maria will stay as late as needed, and most of the kids have settled in now. I'm sure everyone will work together and look out for each other. You're just starting out, don't put so much pressure on yourself."

"You took control of situations when you started here," Aria says. "I want to handle it as quickly as you did."

"I'm a massive control freak," Jazz admits. "You don't want to be like me. You came from an extreme trauma. Be kind to yourself. You're dealing with your own demons. Don't struggle to take on others."

"I guess you're right."

Jazz smiles. "There's no such thing as perfect."

Eddy laughs and then slams a hand over his mouth.

The girls look at him, and he lowers his hand to say, "I'm sorry. It's just I'm so proud of you Jazz, and proud of myself as your therapist."

Gene laughs too, watching the larger-than-life grin on Eddy's face.

The girls hug and then break apart.

"Ari, you know I'm sticking by you," Gene says. "We will get through it together."

Aria sighs, smiling. "Thanks, Genie."

"Oh, hey," Adrian says, stopping by the doorway. "Everyone's in here."

"Just talking about you and Jazz's night out," Gene says.

Adrian walks in and holds his hand out for Jazz. "I wanted to find you and ask if you're ready to leave."

Jazz's eyes brighten as she takes Adrian's hand. "You're ready to leave? *Ha*, I thought I'd have to drag you out of here."

"Maybe I just want to see you all glammed up," Adrian says and kisses her cheek.

Gene sighs. "I wish I could see you guys getting ready. I'd pay to see Adrian in a tux." Gene pulls out his phone and waggles it at

Jazz. "Photos. Yes?"

Jazz winks at him. "Stay logged onto Collage."

Adrian winces. "Really? You're gonna post photos?"

"Get ready, my boy," Jazz says to Adrian, grinning. "You're entering my world that's filled with paparazzi."

"But they won't take photos of me…" Adrian replies hesitantly.

"*Duh*," Gene blurts. "You're on the arm of Jazz Abadi. And you're gorgeous. You'll have flashes all around you."

"Thanks for making me more nervous," Adrian says, tussling Gene's dark curls.

Gene laughs and ducks away from Adrian's hand. "You'll be fine. Jazz will protect you."

Jazz kisses Adrian's cheek. "Sure will. Shall we go?"

"Lead the way," Adrian says. He waves to the others as they leave the room. "Bye guys."

"Bye," Eddy and Aria say.

"Oh, Gene," Jazz says, halfway out the door. "Did you want to talk through the latest information you got with Eddy?"

"What's this?" Eddy asks.

"I'm good," Gene rushes. "Go on, Jazz. Get going."

"You ok, Gene?" Eddy asks.

Why? Because I just learnt my dad is still beating up my mum, even though my leaving was meant to end all of that?

"Nah. I'm good," Gene mumbles. "No idea what Jazz is on about."

Adrian and Jazz left down the hall, hand-in-hand. Eddy and Aria magnetically reconnect into a hug. The same ugly jealousy bubbles inside of Gene.

When am I ever going to find someone? Last night proved I'm too young for the clubs. This sucks.

"I'll catch up with you guys later," Gene says and moves into the hall.

"Did you get the dress?" Tessa whispers, leaning against an exposed brick wall.

Gene nods, his face drooping with a frown.

"She'll meet you in the donations room in an hour," Tessa whispers, and then moves down the opposite end of the hall.

Gene groans. *Great. Everyone else gets to be in love, wrapped up with their special person, and I get Cara. A psycho who can't even call me by the right name.*

Lucky me.

Program

Pippa patrols the gardens by the north wing. Tonight is the Masquerade Ball. The night to have the most activity and renew her sense of purpose in her job. The most noteworthy thing she witnessed today was the event decorators stringing lights amongst the hedges. In other words, Pippa is bored out of her mind.

Voices sound from the rear of the garden. Beyond that corner is no longer her patrol area, but she has an urge to investigate. She creeps around the edge of the building, ears pricked for conversation.

Deacon and another cop, Jenkins, are laughing about this night being worth every penny they've been paid.

Of course, because they're not the ones stuck looking at roses all day.

Deacon's radio sounds off with a message. "New delivery coming through gates."

Deacon and Jenkins move south. Pippa wonders why her radio didn't produce the same message. As she watches the men leave, a van moves from the rear of the property, not the usual service entry for deliveries.

Pippa reasons the van went the wrong way but had the

correct paperwork that passed them through the gates. Curiosity gets the better of her, and she follows Deacon and Jenkins, keeping a safe distance behind them.

After a few twists and turns around the back of the Mansion, a section Pippa did not have a tour through, she spots Deacon and Jenkins meeting the delivery driver.

Odd. Since when do cops handle deliveries? That's for the design and catering teams.

Pippa cranes her neck to get a visual of the opening to the building. She doesn't recognise the area from any of the maps or blueprints she's used to familiarise herself with the building's layout. From what she gathers, it's a non-descript basement entry.

What the hell is going on?

At the back of the van, neon green hair spikes out of the opened door. Pippa's heart squeezes and her blood runs cold.

Neons? Here?

A fingerless leather glove on a tattooed arm emerges, offering a small bag of white powder. Jenkins takes it, examining it and talking with the person in the van.

With a racing heart, Pippa edges against an exterior wall of Walsh Mansion. Her eyes narrow, trying to get a glimpse of the individual in the van.

How many people are in the vehicle? Why are they here? Why are Deacon and Jenkins conversing with them?

Putting her stealth training to its best use, Pippa moves closer, hoping to hear the conversation being held.

"Caden asked for primo stuff," the gravelly voice in the van says. "Is he here to check it out? I have new stuff to show him."

"He's not coming out," Deacon says. "He asked us to take care of it."

"Typical rich kid, not wanting to get their hands dirty," the gravelly voice replies.

Jenkins hands over cash from his back pocket. "Mr Walsh said this will cover what you two discussed at the club. Can you unload into the back of the basement?"

"Sure."

Jenkins and Deacon move away from the van, and they look in Pippa's direction.

Shit!

Pippa turns back toward the garden, hoping they didn't notice her.

"Jackson!" Deacon calls.

"Don't you run!" Jenkins orders. "Get back here."

Pippa halts, a rush of air pouring out of her and her stomach cramping. She turns, shoulders locked, and raises her head to meet their eyes.

The men march towards her.

"What are you doing back here?" Deacon questions sternly. "Why did you leave your post?"

"I heard a commotion back here," Pippa improvises. "I thought it best to check it out or I wouldn't be doing my job."

Jenkins lifts his radio. "You use this and let your colleague at this station know your concerns, and they investigate."

"Are you really so inept at following protocol?" Deacon scolds.

"I'm sorry," Pippa backtracks. "It won't happen again."

"See that it doesn't," Jenkins orders. "Get with the program and get back to your patrol station."

"Inside the house," Deacon adds. "We don't need you in the

garden until nightfall."

"Yes, Sir," Pippa says with gritted teeth. She turns and walks away so nothing flies out of her mouth she will regret.

Proud

Jazz closes her eyes as Marcella applies her eye makeup.

"Did we do it, or did we do it?" Lucas' voice rings behind her.

Jazz feels Marcella move away from her face, and she opens her eyes to see Lucas throwing out his arms in the mirror's reflection. She turns around in her salon chair to see Adrian standing tall in his magnificently tailored tuxedo.

"Adrian," she gushes, her hands clasping in front of her face. "You look so handsome."

"Yes, I think we did it," Lucas cheers, landing his hands on Adrian's shoulders.

Adrian laughs bashfully. "Jazz, you look stunning."

"Thank you," Jazz says, wanting to get out of the chair and wrap her arms around him.

"No dress, yet?" Adrian asks.

Jazz smooths her ivory, silk robe and explains, "Not until after hair and makeup."

"Shall I continue?" Marcella asks, angling her makeup brush towards Jazz.

Jazz nods at Marcella, and Lucas directs Adrian to an adjacent salon chair.

Alberto, Jazz's hair stylist, moves to Adrian's chair, ready to style his hair. Jazz turns to her reflection and admires Alberto's work. He parted her raven hair down the middle and loosely pulled it back into an elegant low bun. The hairstyle directs attention to her teardrop citrine and diamond earrings, which match her necklace pendant.

When Marcella finishes her makeup, Jazz follows Lucas to the dressing room.

"That man of yours will absolutely die when he sees you in this dress," Lucas says, removing the ball gown from its hanger. "He can't get enough of you."

Jazz giggles. "You think so?"

"Oh, hunny, please," Lucas says, throwing his head back. "You're all he can talk about."

Jazz is all smiles as she slips into the dress. Her mind filled with only Adrian.

She stands in front of a three-way mirror as Lucas zips the back. The form-fitting dress, emblazoned with gold detailing, hugs every curve of her body. At her calves, the dress billows out, showing off her strappy gold stilettos.

"You are a goddess, Jazz Abadi," Lucas says in an airy tone.

"Thank you so much for helping us get ready," Jazz says to his reflection. "Tonight is such a monumental event. Not only on the social calendar, but for Adrian and me. It's so nerve-racking, having him meet my father in this setting. But at least we both look the part."

Lucas pats Jazz's shoulder. "There's no way Darius won't approve of Adrian. He will be very proud of you."

Jazz smiles uneasily. "I hope you're right."

Jazz follows Lucas into the salon. Adrian stands from his chair, mouth hanging open.

"He's speechless," Marcella says in awe.

Jazz stands before Adrian, her grin hurting her cheeks, and sweeps his hands into hers. "Hi," she whispers.

"Hi," he whispers back, his smile growing.

"You two are just the cutest," Marcella says, still aweing.

"Your car is pulling up," Alberto says by the window.

Marcella approaches Jazz with a gold mask. "Don't forget this."

Tingles spread through Jazz's veins as Marcella ties the mask above her bun. Alberto fixes Adrian's black mask, the last checkbox marked for the Masquerade Ball.

"Excited?" Jazz asks, gesturing to the door.

Adrian nods, unable to take his eyes off her. "Yes. More excited than I expected. I'm so lucky to be with you."

Jazz kisses him quickly. "Not as lucky as me. I love you."

In a hush, he replies, "I love you more."

They leave the salon, hand-in-hand, and as the car pulls to a stop, Adrian jerks back.

"A limo?" he asks, and Jazz senses his trepidation.

She laces her fingers with his. "You're with me, remember. It's not about anybody else. It's you and me tonight. The place may be littered with rich snobs, but we will be ok because we will be together."

Adrian smiles and relaxes. He steps forward and opens the car door for Jazz, before the driver can get to it. Jazz nods to the driver to return to the car. She slides into the backseat the best she can in her body-hugging dress.

"You look so incredible," Adrian says, sliding in beside her.

"But I hope you know it's you, not the dress, I'm *gaga* over. Your personality, integrity, courage, strength. They are the reasons I'm lucky to be with you, not just your beauty." He smiles cheekily. "Even though beauty is pretty high on the list."

Jazz gently wipes under her masked eye. She lightly sniffs and smiles. "You're such a wonderful man. So honest, and kind, and respectful. I'm so grateful fate brought us together, no matter how surreal the circumstances."

They stare longingly into each other's eyes until the surge of emotion gets the better of Jazz. Her love, attraction, and closeness to Adrian lights a fire inside her. She needs him now. She grabs onto his tie and suctions her lips to his, their masks clunking together. His hand slides around her back and camps between her shoulder blades. Jazz slides a hand along the side of Adrian's face and lays more passion into her kiss. She wishes her dress wasn't so constricting so she could toss a leg over him. She presses her body against his and runs a hand into his gorgeously styled hair.

Adrian pulls his lips away with a faint laugh. "Aren't you worried about messing up our hair or clothes?"

Jazz touches a finger to her probably messed up lipstick and laughs. She's giddy as she replies, "No. No, I'm not. That's so weird."

"You're loosening up, Miss Abadi."

"You're rubbing off on me, Mr Cassidy."

Jazz giggles and brings her lips closer to his. She presses her lips on his and feels every ounce of love pump her heart.

As the limousine climbs the wide and winding road into Sovereign Hill, its speed decreases, flowing into the line of vehicles ready to pull into Walsh Mansion.

Jazz checks her makeup in the compact mirror from her gold-beaded clutch purse, and she smiles. "Wow, Marcella did a great job. Everything is still in place."

Adrian kisses her cheek. "You are flawless."

Jazz closes the mirror and lets out a wispy laugh. "You're too much." She looks out the tinted window to the press lining the pavement and the flashes of paparazzi photographers. "You still want to do this?"

"I have something for you that might answer that."

Jazz turns from the window as Adrian retrieves a piece of paper from his jacket pocket. He hands it to her, and she takes it with interest.

As she unfolds the paper, her hands tremble and heart pounds. In large, uncertain characters is a handwritten note.

Jazz. I love you. You are my world. I want to be with you forever.

Jazz's mouth falls open as she looks at Adrian. "You wrote this?"

His smile is small, his eyes shine, and he nods.

Jazz leans into him, running her arms around his shoulders. "I love it. Thank you so much. I'm so proud of you."

"I know it's not much," he whispers.

"Stop. It's fantastic. I know how hard you struggled." Her eyes well with pride. "How did you manage it so neatly?"

"Cara helped me."

Jazz's heart sinks slightly. "Oh. That's wonderful. I'm glad. It's a fantastic surprise."

"You look disappointed."

Jazz quickly grows her smile. "I'm not. Truly, I'm not."

"I wanted her help so I could surprise you."

"Thank you."

"Do you wish it was only you that helped me?"

Jazz kisses him and then whispers, "No. If she helped you learn, I'm happy. I know I'm not the first person to teach you. We have more to our relationship than reading and writing."

Adrian smiles and kisses her back. "That we do."

When their limousine stops at the red carpet, Jazz and Adrian take steady breaths in and out as their driver moves to their door. Flashes of light bombard them, after the safety of the tinted window is removed. Jazz exits the car first, and a crowd cheers her name. She smiles and turns to Adrian, taking his hand as he leaves the vehicle.

They walk the red carpet and Jazz smiles as the press calls her name. She squeezes Adrian's hand, signalling to stop for a picture. With an uneasy expression, Adrian stands by her. His hand slips behind her back. She leans into him and they pose for an onslaught of flashes.

After two minutes, Jazz leads Adrian by the hand to the entrance of Walsh Mansion. She doesn't stop for questions, only responding in smiles.

At the entrance, a server greets them with a tray of bubbling champagne glasses. Jazz takes a glass and Adrian declines. She brushes his cheek as his complexion pales.

She pulls him off to the side, rubbing his arm and searching his eyes. "How are you doing?"

"That was a lot," he whispers.

"I'm sorry. If this gets too much, we can leave."

"No," he says, smiling and squeezing her hand. "No, I want to do this. I want to be with you. In your world. You've adapted to mine, it's the least I can do."

"Your world is my world now. I don't need this."

"You enjoyed getting dressed up today. You've been looking forward to tonight. I won't take it away from you."

Jazz kisses his cheek, feeling her heart swell. "You're amazing."

"I'll do anything for you, Jazz."

Lovesick, Jazz is sure her heart will soon pop out of her dress.

Mission

Cara pushes open the door to the donations room and finds Gene in the middle of the floor. He busily sews large pockets into a big blue puffball.

"Oh, hell, no," Cara says, staring at the dress. "That's what she got me?"

"Ungrateful much?" Gene mutters. "I would die to go to this event. All you do is be an absolute bitch and you weasel your way in."

Cara smirks as she plops down beside him. "Jealous much?"

"*Ha ha,*" he grimaces and continues to sew.

Cara feels the pocket material between her fingers. "That feels very sturdy."

Gene nods to a chest of drawers. "I just cut up the ugliest clothes we had. Better hidden away in a ball gown than never worn."

"Thanks," Cara says, grinning.

Gene eyes her sceptically.

Cara nods, smiling pleasantly. "Seriously. Thank you for your hard work."

"Whatever."

Cara stands and peels off her jacket. "Think I'll be able to blend in with these snobs?"

"Nope."

"Thanks for the faith."

Gene stands, lifting the dress with him. "But thankfully you have me. And I can turn the biggest dirt pile into a princess."

Cara points to her chest. "I'm the dirt pile."

"Yes, you're the dirt pile." Gene tilts his head as he looks her up and down. "Did you shower today?"

"Good lord," Cara grizzles. "Just give me the damn dress, would ya."

Cara snatches the dress from Gene and unbuckles her jeans.

"*Arghh!*" Gene yelps, throwing his hands up and turning away. "There's a divider you can go behind and change."

"Oh, calm down," Cara says, slipping out of her jeans. "Neither of us are interested in what the other is selling. Stop being such a baby."

"It's incredible how nice you are to people who are helping you," Gene says sarcastically, keeping his back turned against her.

"Wait," Cara says, pulling the dress to her hips. "This is strapless?"

"What's wrong with that?"

"What do I wear underneath it?"

Gene turns around to see her thick black crop top. He moves over to her and lifts the dress up her waist and over her chest.

"Oh boy. That's not gonna work."

Cara frowns. "No shit."

"I guess Jazz assumed you had the correct underwear."

"Why would she assume that?"

"Because she has everything. She's never been on the streets with no belongings before."

"Hold on to the dress while I take this top off."

"*Eww.*"

"*Ugh.* Just do it."

"Ok, ok."

Cara pulls the crop top up and over her head, and Gene lifts the dress over her bustline. He moves behind her and clasps the long line of buttons.

"I'll add some thin straps to the dress," Gene says. "It won't take much time at all."

"I'm sorry you're not going tonight," Cara whispers. "Why didn't you ask Jazz for a ticket?"

"I never thought to," Gene says behind her. "Tonight is a big deal for her and Adrian. All I thought about was how they'd prepare and get through it. I never thought of getting myself in."

"I think she should have known to get you a ticket. You obviously love this stuff. The culture, the clothes, following the people. If I had the money, I would buy you a ticket."

"*Pfft.* You would not. Besides, it's easy to say when you don't have the money."

"And you say I'm not nice."

Gene pulls Cara's hair out of its messy ponytail.

"Hey!" she yelps in defence.

"I gotta do your hair. You won't get in with this bird's nest." He walks around her. "Are you sure you'll be able to carry things inside your dress?"

Cara slides her hand inside the dress to access the biggest pocket. "I'll handle it."

"Max thinks you're going as a revenge plot against the Mayor."

"He can think whatever he likes. I'm just doing my job."

"I'm going to my room to get some stuff," Gene says, moving to the door. "Be back in a minute."

Alone in the room, Cara stands in front of the floor-length mirror. Her hands smooth over the constricted bodice, and her eyes are dazzled by the lace layered over the bouffant skirt. Rosettes and ribbons belt her waist in three shades of pale blues. The delicate glitter detailing throughout the blue ball gown overwhelms her.

Who is this girl?

Gene re-enters with a black canvas backpack.

"Hey, I remember that," Cara says, reaching for the tear from a barbed wire of a back alley fence.

Gene yanks the bag away. "Don't touch."

Cara holds her hands up. "Yes, Sir. I remember how precious you are about that thing. What you got in it, anyway?"

"My best products... that I cannot believe I'm using on you."

Irritation festers inside Cara. She glares at him and swears that one more smart-arse remark and she will strangle him. She's done it before, and even in this balloon of a dress, it will be just as simple.

Gene moves behind her and starts spraying something with a coconut scent into her hair. It's too sweet, and she doesn't like it. She winces as the sticky product lands on her forehead. He roughly brushes her hair, jolting her head back with the strokes.

"Your hair is so knotty. We should have started a lot earlier."

"I needed Adrian out of the building," Cara mumbles.

"Why didn't you tell him you'll be there? He'll recognise you, won't he?"

"*Duh*, there's a mask around here, isn't there?"

"Yeah, your mask and heels are over there in the corner."

Cara's breath clogs in her throat. "*Heels*?"

"Yeah. You're wearing a ball gown and going to Walsh Mansion. Heels are non-negotiable."

"How am I supposed to sneak around in high heels?"

"Should have gotten a lesson from Jazz. She does it all the time," Gene says smugly.

"Well, she's just freaking perfect, isn't she?"

"Yes," Gene says, grinning. "She is."

Cara's eyes somersault.

"I'll keep your hair down at the back, so it covers this," Gene says, touching her mark below her neck.

Cara flinches. "Don't touch it."

"Sorry." Gene separates her hair into pieces and sighs heavily. "I wish you weren't doing this. You know it's more than just a fancy party upstairs."

"What are you talking about?"

"There's gonna be this creepy gambling, drug-fuelled, strip club vibe thing going on downstairs."

Cara rips her hair away from Gene as she whips her head around. "Are you on drugs right now? What are you blabbering about?"

Gene rolls his eyes and huffs. "I'm trying to warn you."

"Warn me about what?"

"I overheard these guy's last night in a club. The Mayor's son organised the Neons to bring drugs to the Mansion for a party in his basement. All the university crowd is invited."

Cara's teeth grit as infuriation plunders her veins. Her hand shoots up and latches around Gene's neck and her fingernails pierce his skin. "Are you telling me," she says in a low, menacing tone, "that you went back into the Nightclub District after I told you not to?"

Gene gasps and chokes, swatting his hands against her powerful arm.

Cara lets him go, and he stumbles, leaning forward as he coughs and splutters.

"Spit it out!" she orders.

Gene rubs his throat, his cheeks red and his forehead sweat-soaked.

She steps forward, glaring and towering over him.

"Yes, I went back there," he yells, shoving her backward. "Don't you dare touch me again."

"You put yourself in a situation directly involving the Neons. You are being so stupid."

"It's what you're doing!"

"It's my life. I have a deal with the Neons. They don't owe you anything. You're a prime target for them. Why won't you believe me?"

"Nothing bad happened!" Gene yells at her, his throat burning. "I was just trying to warn you! But forget it, you horrid cow!"

Cara stares at him, unblinking.

"You're yelling at me," she deadpans.

Gene tilts his head, grimacing. "What is wrong with you? You attacked me. Of course, I'm yelling."

"So, the same people I pick the pockets of in the clubs will be at the Mansion. You thought that was bad news for me?" Cara asks, her emotions deadened.

Gene's mouth hangs open, uttering nonsensical sounds.

"These people are proven easy targets. This is good news, Pee-Brain." Cara huffs and shifts her dress across her chest. "There's a second party in the basement? Why would they do that? I thought these rich people liked to put on a big show."

Gene groans and works on her in frustration. "That's my point, Freakshow. There's some shady business going on that you're not prepared for."

"*Ouch.* Watch it, would ya," Cara grumbles as Gene tugs at her hair. "I'm ready for everything. There's nothing they can do I haven't seen before."

"You are so conceited."

"Hey, these kids went to the school for the rich. I went to the school for trouble. They can't outplay me."

"Why am I even helping you?"

"Kid, thank you for letting me know," Cara says. "At least I know where to target now."

Gene yelps. "Are you serious! I was warning you, not telling you a plan. Why would you go there?"

"It's gambling, AKA money. And drugs I can sell back to the Neons. Talk about a payday."

Gene groans. "I'm done talking to you."

"*Pfft.* You love me."

"*Ha!*"

"We've called for your car," Tessa says when she and Max enter the room. "Should be here in twenty minutes."

"We have a deal," Max says, pointing squarely at Cara. "I've helped you with this, so you don't tell Dean where I am."

"Yeah, yeah," Cara says, wincing as Gene brutally works a

comb through her hair. "We never met."

Max grins. "Awesome. Good luck tonight."

"Thanks. I won't need it."

"Take the luck, Girl," Tessa says. "This is a high security mission. If you pull this off, I'll be floored."

Cara scoffs. "Thanks for the confidence."

"Just don't get yourself killed," Gene murmurs.

"*Killed*?" Cara says disbelievingly. "Trust me, in this getup, I won't stick out."

"Eddy's in his office with someone," Max says. "And Aria is talking with people in the common room about yesterday's press conference. You've got time to sneak out of here."

"In that case, you'd better start walking in heels," Gene says, twisting Cara's hair. "I've just a few locks to pin back and then you can practice until your car arrives."

Tessa backs away. "You guys can do that on your own."

"So much for women having each other's back," Cara says, flinching each time Gene jams a pin against the back of her head.

"You'll be right," Tessa smirks. "Use some of those cat burglar skills you talk up so much."

Cara rolls her eyes, ready to master the shoes to keep her confidence alive.

Happy

Jazz and Adrian follow a server to their designated table. On the way, a striking young woman with silky, strawberry blonde hair and a bubble-gum pink ball gown grabs Jazz's attention.

"Jazz Abadi?" she says, reaching for Jazz.

"Yes?" Jazz replies, and the girl drops her hand.

"Ah, hi," the girl says with a wide grin and a blush to match her dress. Botox has frozen her blemish free skin, and her lips are plump with fillers. "My name is Rory Briar. I just wanted to say hi. I've been an admirer of yours for forever."

"Oh, that's so sweet of you," Jazz replies, knowing the girl is referring to her social media ranking and not her philanthropy.

"I go to MC University, but we never seemed to run in the same circles. And then I heard you graduated early."

Jazz nods. "I wasn't in the party scene."

She smiles, playing with a shiny lock of her hair. "Yeah, I got that. But your following was through the roof." Rory pulls her phone from her clutch purse. "Would you take a selfie with me? Do you mind if I post it to Collage?"

Jazz nods. "That's fine. I'm sure you'll have more followers than me soon enough. I don't post nearly as often."

"I wish. You rule on the platform." Rory holds her phone high, and Jazz poses beside her. "Thank you so much, Jazz."

"No problem, Rory. What are you studying?"

"You'll think it's dumb."

"Try me."

"Early Childhood Care. I really love children." Rory's nervous energy bounces. "Does it go right over your head if something's not business-related?"

Jazz clutches Rory's hand and smiles warmly. "Not at all. I think it's wonderful."

Rory smiles. "Thank you. I should let you go to your table." She nods over Jazz's shoulder. "This is your date?"

Jazz turns, smiling. "Yes, this is Adrian."

Rory holds out her hand daintily towards Adrian. "Charmed."

Adrian awkwardly shakes Rory's hand, which she angled expecting him to kiss the back of it.

"I'd best be moving on," Rory says. "Have you seen Caden?"

"No, not yet," Jazz answers.

"I heard he likes pink," she says with a giggle.

"Have a good time, Rory," Jazz says. "Just be careful who you socialise with."

"Don't worry about me. My focus tonight is on the most eligible bachelor here." She waves goodbye, and her dress swishes as she moves around the tables.

"I've never seen someone look so plastic," Adrian mutters.

Jazz cups a hand over her mouth before a laugh can escape. "Honestly, that was nothing. Wait until you see some of the older ladies here."

Adrian cringes. "Would you ever get plastic surgery?"

"*Ehck*, no," Jazz retches. "This face and body will never be tampered with."

Adrian grins and kisses her cheek. "Good."

The server stands ahead of them, gesturing to a table. Jazz takes Adrian's hand as they approach. She gazes around the table, recognising her dear friend Sachi Yuki and her parents. She waves to them, and then her nerves rattle as her father rises from his seat.

Darius steps forward. His greying hair slicked back, his evening suit impeccable, and his arms out wide. "My precious daughter."

She lets go of Adrian's hand and embraces her father. "Good to see you. You look well."

"You too." Darius chortles. "We live in the same house and rarely see one another. Life gets too busy."

"We need to rectify that. Make time for one another."

Darius smiles brightly. "Agreed."

Jazz turns back to Adrian. "Father, do you remember Adrian?"

"Not well, I must admit," Darius says, and shakes Adrian's hand. "How do you do?"

"Good, thank you," Adrian says nervously. "And you?"

"As well as can be expected," Darius replies, the wrinkles deepening under his eyes. "It won't be a late evening for me, I'm afraid."

"You've made an appearance," Jazz says, smiling at her father's unmasked face. "They can't ask any more of you."

Darius brushes her cheek. "You look beautiful, my dear."

"Thank you."

"And your beau looks better than I imagined," Darius says with a chuckle. "The way people talk about you, I expected a street urchin."

"A what?" Adrian asks, startled.

Jazz smiles and rubs Adrian's arm. "Don't take any notice. Father's just having some fun."

"Ok?" Adrian replies.

"*Jazz!*" Sachi squeals, racing towards her and throwing her arms around her.

Jazz giggles. "Hello, gorgeous. How are you? You look stunning."

"Why, thank you," Sachi says, grinning as she poses in her ruffled black and white evening gown. "I feel stunning. And you. What a knockout of a dress."

"Thank you. Sachi, this is my boyfriend, Adrian," Jazz introduces. "I've known Sachi since she was a baby."

"She acts like she's so much older than me," Sachi teases.

"It was only a few months ago I attended your sweet sixteen party."

Sachi shakes Adrian's hand. "It's nice to meet you. So glad to see someone helping Jazz stay grounded."

"Nice to meet you too. And it's all her putting in the hard work."

Darius cups Jazz's hand in his. "Will you grant me one dance?"

"Of course, Father." She looks at Adrian. "Do you mind?"

"No, not at all. Please, go ahead."

"Thank you." She winks at Sachi. "We'll catch up later."

"I won't keep her long," Darius says with a jovial smile.

Jazz lets her father lead her onto the dancefloor. When they commence dancing, she says, "You seem in a rather good mood tonight."

"Seeing my daughter happy will do that."

"I am happy."

"He seems like a fine young man."

"He is. I love him very much."

"You understand, I don't care about his financial situation."

"You don't?"

"I didn't come from money. I met your mother, who also didn't come from money. We fell deeply in love and made a very happy life. That is all I want for you, my dearest. Happiness."

Jazz's eyes tear up. "Oh, Father."

"It makes me realise, I don't think I ever saw you happy before."

"No, that can't be true."

"You weren't as blissful until that boy came into your life."

Jazz smiles, believing it to be true.

"I don't want you to go back to Ultimate ME."

Jazz's smile drops. "What?"

"Ultimate ME didn't make you happy. You are doing tremendous work now. You feel fulfilled, yes?"

She nods. "Yes."

"And you are in love?"

She grins. "Yes."

"You stay where you are. Run the non-profit. You help people in distress and make your mother and I proud."

Jazz grips her father's hand and shoulder tightly, her knees buckling. "You really think I'm making Mother proud?"

"I know it," he whispers soothingly. "She is more present with me now than ever. You are a miracle, Jazz."

A tear slips from her eye. Her mother's image fills her vision.

"Thank you. You don't know how much I've needed to hear that."

They stand in place. Darius smooths back Jazz's hair, looking at her tenderly.

"I'm so glad to see you tonight," he says. "But I should go to my table to rest."

"I'll walk you back," Jazz says, linking her arm with his.

"Miss Abadi," Ethan's voice cuts through.

Jazz looks ahead to see Ethan Roth walking towards them.

"Lovely to see you. All Darius has spoken of all week is seeing you tonight." Ethan takes Jazz's hand and kisses it. "And you haven't disappointed. You look absolutely divine, Jazz. How are you?"

Jazz takes her hand back. "I'm fine. How are you, Ethan?"

"Busy as always." He gestures behind her. "Care to dance?"

"I'm walking my father back to his seat."

"No, no," Darius says, unravelling his arm from Jazz's. "I'm more than capable of walking myself back. Please, go ahead."

Ugh.

She flashes Ethan her fakest smile as he takes her hand again.

"Don't get surly with me," Ethan says, wrapping his arm around her back and lifting her hand high with his other. "I'm trying to be civil with you."

"I'm not interested in any of your games."

Ethan tilts his head, smiling. "Jazz, I'm not interested in playing with you tonight. Caden's already organised all the games I need."

Jazz's eyes slit at the pompous smirk on Ethan's lips.

I thought he was too grown up to hang around Caden Walsh. Only a few months ago, at my graduation dinner, he was acting too superior to sit by the pool with us.

"Keep whatever Caden's organised to yourself," Jazz says, clamping her hand around Ethan's. "I don't want to know about it."

"Abadi, *geez*," Ethan whines. "You're crushing my hand."

Jazz smiles, alleviating her pressure. "Just making my point, Roth."

"So, thought more about coming back to the company to head the social media department?"

"How many times do I have to tell you no?"

He laughs. "Ok, fine."

"Just ensure to keep the executive level multicultural," she says. "You know how important that is to my father. He capitalised ME to remind himself where he came from. Leaving the Middle East with nothing to his name. If you are leading this company, it's your duty to ensure people of colour help you run it."

"You know I will. But it doesn't explain why you won't run it with me."

"You haven't regained my trust. Nevermind the fact I've found fulfilment elsewhere."

"You can't put lipstick on a pig, Abadi."

"Are you trying to describe Adrian, or getting confused and talking about yourself?"

Ethan throws his head back in laughter. "Oh, I've missed you. I forgot how much you infuriate me."

Decorum

Cara perches on the backseat of the limousine, peering out the darkened window. The vehicle's snail pace drives Cara to aggravation.

"Can't this thing go any faster?" she shouts at the driver.

"We are backed up," the driver replies. "Same thing every year. Madness. Everyone poses for photos and slows down the entire line."

Cara pulls on the door handle. "I'm just gonna walk."

"You can't do that. No one walks the street."

"What does it matter? I need to beat this line."

"It's not proper," the driver reasons.

Cara smirks. "Nothing about me is proper."

Cara exits the car and pulls her dress above her ankles. She marches the hill to Walsh Mansion with instant regret.

Damn these high heels.

Cara breathes through the pain as her toes slide forward in her shoes and scrunch together. The cement pounds through her heels and into her ankles. She grits her teeth and keeps moving to the high brass gate of Walsh Mansion. She passes a limousine, and a window rolls down. A distinct hiss of disapproval flies at Cara.

Laughter rolls out of Cara, enjoying the gasps of shock from the snooty couples.

Her shoulders seize up. *What if Jazz and Adrian are in one of these cars? Will they know it's me? Who else would walk instead of staying in their car? Jazz will recognise the dress and tell Adrian. That's if she hasn't already...*

Does Adrian know I'm coming?

Crap.

Cara pushes past a posing couple at the top of the red carpet. Photographers call, asking for her name, but Cara pushes forward to the entrance.

A man at the entrance holds out his hand like a stop sign. "Invitation?"

Cara presents her invitation with the cheeriest smile she can muster.

Maybe walking was the worst idea. Everyone will suspect a girl with no decorum.

"Welcome, Miss Cassidy," the man says, reading the invitation.

Cara's eyebrow arches as he hands the invitation back.

"Thank you," she murmurs and walks into the foyer. She looks down at the invitation. In calligraphy, states *Cara Cassidy*.

Cara didn't read the invitation Jazz left with the dress, not expecting a personalised name. A quiver lingers in her throat. She doesn't know what her real name is, but she loves looking at this name. The smile playing at her lips lifts her spirits.

She tucks the invitation in a pocket of her dress. Making her way inside the building, she internally squashes any remaining emotion. The sheer size of the ballroom is overwhelming. Three giant crystal chandeliers hang from the high, vaulted ceiling. Large round tables scatter the outer edges, and in the centre sits the glossy, herringbone dancefloor.

Men in three-piece evening suits and women in spectacular ball gowns waltz together. Cara scans the couples, noting the non-existence of same-sex couples. Her stomach twists and her skin crawls. Being in the room is a level far above uncomfortable.

She adjusts her blue beaded mask and moves between groups of people. With ease, she picks a pearl bracelet, a loose-fitting diamond ring, two men's wallets, and a pair of cufflinks. Mingling people are too busy with their champagne flutes and gossip to notice. She tucks the items into her side pocket and spies for more access of Walsh Mansion.

This is like a club haul on steroids.

Her jaw tightens at the sight of Mayor Walsh at the head table. He swigs red wine and laughs boisterously with other politicians.

He's so concerned with himself, he'll never see what I'm doing right under his nose.

Mask

Adrian walks the edge of the dancefloor as Jazz dances with her father. Taking in the crowd, he stands tall, trying to belong. Jazz gave him a top quality suit and the best stylist. By all accounts, he's no less than anyone else in the room.

I belong?

He laughs at himself.

No way. I do not belong.

Smiling, he takes another glance around the room. His smile diminishes as a girl in a blue dress steals his attention. She has neat blonde hair, a blue mask covers half her face, and her dress balloons around her. Despite all this, it's the way she moves that captivates him. Her shoulders stay square, her elbows locked, gathering the sides of her dress, ready to flee at a moment's notice. She sails around the other guests unnoticed.

What the hell?

How...

Why is Cara here?

Without another question, Adrian moves into the crowd, towards the girl.

"Hey," he says, reaching out and clutching her arm.

"What?" Cara says, turning and gasping as she sees him.

"What are you doing here?"

"You're mistaking me for someone else."

"Don't play with me. How'd you think I wouldn't recognise you?" Adrian whispers harshly, his grip intensifying around Cara's arm.

"Let go off me," Cara whispers stubbornly.

"Tell me what you're doing here. How did you get in?" He looks her up and down. "Where did you get the dress?"

"This is my kinda place, Bro," Cara smirks, straightening her mask. "You know I like disguises."

"What are you up to?"

"Stop interrogating me. Go back to your date. I thought she was most important to you now."

"My relationship is important, but that doesn't make you any less. You're getting yourself into trouble. Stop whatever you're planning."

"You forget, Adrian," she hisses, yanking her arm free. "They marked me trouble at birth. This is what I live for."

Cara turns in her ball gown and swiftly moves away from him.

Adrian's jaw clenches as Cara disappears into the crowd. His gut clamps as he decides not to follow her.

There's no reasoning with her.

Unenthused, he moves across the floor to where he left Jazz. He looks through the dancefloor to find her and stops dead.

Ethan?

He blinks and squints to ensure his mind isn't playing tricks on him.

There's no mistaking it. Jazz is dancing with Ethan Roth. The man who tried to control her and force her into marriage.

"Hell no!" It bursts out of him. He barges onto the dancefloor, weaving between twirling couples, and marches towards Jazz and Ethan.

Jazz spots him over Ethan's shoulder. Her face is a mixture of embarrassment and apology.

Ethan notices Jazz's focus and turns to lock eyes with Adrian. "Yes?" Ethan asks, bothered.

Adrian ignores Ethan, who deserves less. His eye contact remains with Jazz. He extends his hand, and asks, "May I have this dance, Miss?"

Jazz grins and pushes away from Ethan. "Excuse me, Ethan, I have to dance with the man of my dreams."

Ethan steps aside, and Adrian and Jazz embrace like they are the only two in the room.

A few steps away, Jazz clears her throat and says, "I was dancing with him to not upset my father."

"I'm not mad at you."

Nervous laughter rushes out of her. "Oh, good."

"You're never at fault when it involves him."

"He wasn't being harmful. I was just ensuring he's keeping my father calm and stable at work." Jazz shrugs. "They both think their work relationship is moving forward strongly."

"Are you ok with that?"

"I'm ok with that." Jazz smiles. "My father approves. He approves of me working at the shelter. He approves of you. Of us."

Adrian smiles with surprise. "Really? He doesn't want you to find someone better?"

Jazz leans in and kisses him. "There's no one better."

Adrian's floating. When he realises his feet are in fact on the ground, he laughs. "I don't know what I'm doing here. You have to show me how to do this."

Jazz squeals with delight. "I would always get in trouble for leading. Now my date wants me to."

"You know I like it when you take charge. From day one, I learnt you're not a follower."

"Ok, this hand on my back, and place it under my shoulder blade," Jazz instructs. "And our clasped hands want to sit in the air right about here."

Adrian tries to steady his hands where Jazz has positioned them. Already feeling flustered, and they have yet to get to the feet.

"There's a box step we should do," Jazz tells, "but let's just move in a slow circle. All we need to do is stay close."

"You can teach me the steps."

"I'm too mesmerised by your eyes to worry about teaching."

"Is that why our reading lessons take so long?" Adrian jokes.

Jazz laughs. "Are you saying I'm a bad teacher?"

Adrian kisses her quickly. "No way. It'll take our whole lives for me to learn."

"That can be arranged," Jazz says, giddy. "Ready to add in a dance move?"

"Sure."

"Hold your hand up and spin me out." Jazz spins out, and then she says, "Spin me back."

Adrian spins her back, and as she reaches him, he dips her backwards and kisses her lips.

Jazz's smile spreads as he removes his lips. "How did you know to do that?" she asks, cradled in his arms.

Adrian pulls her up, smiling. "Movies."

Jazz giggles and places her hand on his shoulder, and they continue in a small, slow circle.

Adrian nestles his head by Jazz's. His smile is immovable. The encounter with his sister the furthest thing from his mind.

Girls

Caden sits by his father, for appearance's sake. The Masquerade Ball is as dull as he expected. The only positive is finding some fine-looking ladies to take downstairs with him.

Or leave them upstairs waiting for me...

"Remember what we talked about, Caden?" his father says, swirling a glass of merlot.

"Huh?" Caden replies with little interest.

"Finding a woman suitable to sit at this table with us," his father elaborates.

Boooooring!

"You'll be out of university soon. We need you out of the party scene and acting like a respectable member of society."

"My last name is Walsh. I'm already set."

"That means nothing. We've banished Walshs before."

"That old story again," Caden says, bored out of his mind. "I don't see any proof to that tall tale."

"I've worked hard to get where I am, and even harder to make an easy transition for you to takeover. Why must you be so ungrateful?"

Caden stands, grabbing a glass of scotch from a server's silver tray. He takes a sip and then says to his father, "Guess I was just born this way."

He moves away from the table and mingles with the guests. He bypasses older guests like plague victims. Young men praise him and wink acknowledgment of the downstairs frivolities. Caden swaggers his way around the young women, all vying for his attention.

He takes two women by the hand and pulls them from the group. One with pearly white teeth and beautiful ebony skin that sends his knees weak. The other with toffee-coloured skin and a light dusting of glitter, tempting him to bed her right away.

He kisses both on the cheek, and says, "Go into the hall and follow until you reach a winding, oak staircase. Go upstairs and tell the guards your Caden's girls. They'll show you to my suite."

The girls look at each other, mystified.

Caden's charisma-soaked smile captivates his prey. "Trust me. It'll be worth it."

Obligingly, the girls nod. Linking arms, they move towards the hall.

Too easy.

Deciding his other party needs him, he slips past the guests and exits the ballroom. On his way, he spies a pretty little number in a bubble-gum pink dress. Her shiny botoxed face and angelic blond hair grabs his attention. She waves at him, coyly. He laughs, smiles, and waves back.

Rory Briar. Any frat parties she's attended, she's been a good girl. A total wet blanket. She'd be zero fun downstairs.

"It's been a long time since I was at a frat house," Ethan Roth says, patting Caden's back as he enters the basement party. "This had better be worth my while."

"*Please.* I'm not holding some basic frat party," Caden says, straightening his velvet jacket. "What do you take me for?"

"Forgive me for not seeing you for more than the child you are."

Oh man, this guy had better get out of my face.

"Ethan, why don't you relax and play some poker?" Caden says, wanting this stuffed shirt away from him.

Ethan huffs and clicks his fingers at a server, ordering a single-malt scotch with one ice cube.

"Angelina," Caden calls. As Angelina sways her hips towards him, Caden gestures towards Ethan. "Angelina, baby, please tend to my dear friend Mr Roth and ensure he has a good time."

"Sure thing, sweetie-pie," Angelina says, looping her arm around Ethan's. "How you doing, hunny?"

Ethan grins at Angelina's chest. "Fantastic."

"Ok, Roth, you're all set," Caden says, hurrying in the opposite direction of the pair.

Caden moves over to his lads, Henry, Tyler, and Derek. His VIPs with the best table and card dealer. "Lads, how's the night treating you?"

"Why is Angelina all over Ethan?" Tyler asks, pouting.

"Don't whine," Caden replies. "I just gave her to Ethan to shut him up. Don't you start with me."

"Caden, this party is baller," Henry cheers. "I can't believe your dad has no clue."

"I know," Caden says, annoyed. "What do I have to do for a little attention?"

"A little?" Derek splutters. "Ah, dude, you've got all of Province in your basement."

"Yeah, and so what? Nothing will come from it," Caden says, stealing Tyler's vodka rocks. "Even with you knuckleheads blabbing about tonight all over town."

"What are you looking for?" Henry asks, puzzled. "Why are you never satisfied?"

Caden ignores the question and scans the room for talent. He moves away from the table, grinning ear to ear.

"Officer Hot Body," he cheers. "You came!"

Officer Jackson jolts, startled by him. "Mr Walsh. I was on patrol and checking in."

"Please," Caden says, welcomingly. "Come in and make yourself comfortable."

"Mr Walsh, I'm on duty. Please don't address me like one of your guests."

"But you are my guest. I want you to be here. You don't have to be such a prude."

"Believe me, you don't want me."

Caden's laugh erupts from his belly. "You are too much. Saying those things only makes me want you more."

Pippa *tsks* and steps away from him. "I should get back to my post."

"I'll find you later," Caden says with a wink.

"Only if you want to be in handcuffs. And not in the fun way," Pippa calls as she walks away.

"You're too much. I'm going to get you, you have my word."

"You don't know how much you'll regret that."

"*Pa-ha*! Whatever," Caden calls back, turning back to his

guests.

"Sir," Deacon says, marching towards him. "What were you and Jackson discussing?"

"Just a bit of cat and mouse. Nothing to report, yet."

"Don't engage with her, Sir."

"What are you talking about?"

"She's not on the payroll, if you catch my drift. We have reason to believe she's scaling an investigation on you. Don't give her any ammunition."

"An investigation? On me?" Caden says, dumbfounded. "That's ridiculous. No one goes after me. What would she gain?"

"That's why we believe Jackson is dangerous. She was assigned to the Mansion so we can keep tabs on her and figure out who she's working for."

Caden's good mood dies. "Is she working for someone trying to steal the top job from my dad?"

"There are several possibilities, Sir."

Caden's hand twists into a fist. "She's going down."

"What do you want me to do?"

"Get me a drink," Caden says, stretching his neck. "I need a mood booster. I want everyone to have a good time. We'll sort out Jackson afterwards."

"I'll radio Jenkins to ensure she's back at her post. We can't have her snooping around."

"Maybe get her back here and I'll keep an eye on her," Caden suggests. "I can always turn a girl around."

"Let Jenkins handle her," Deacon says. "I'll get you that drink."

You'll regret that. Suddenly Officer Jackson's words have a whole new meaning to them.

No, Jackson, you'll learn to regret messing with me.

Mystery

Cara stalks the ballroom, looking for a direct route out of the room. On her way in, she noticed guards blocking the opposite route from the foyer. Police officers in black suits patrol the halls. Guests pass them without an issue, but how far will posing as a lost socialite get her?

Where's the underground entrance? It has to be somewhere out of sight so the oldies don't see it, but clear enough the kids know where to go.

Is there a secret password or something?

She nears glass double doors, and moves through onto a tiled balcony, letting the crisp night air refresh her. Across the balcony, stone steps lead down into a garden. She sails down, hopeful for a path leading to a lower entrance.

The garden path winds around hedges and soon enough she is surrounded by roses, twinkle lights, and stone benches.

The underground party must be on the other side of this garden.

"Miss?" a female voice calls. "Are you ok? Do you need help finding where to go?"

Cara fixes her mask and turns to the voice. Her mouth falls open as a beautiful woman stands before her.

Gorgeous tanned complexion. Strong angles to her face. Softly pinned back brunette curls. A sexy black suit, crisp white blouse, and a skinny black tie.

Pippa.

"No, thank you," Cara says with a fake, bubbly voice. "I'm going back inside."

"I'll walk you back," Pippa offers.

"No, really," Cara blurts, lifting her hands. She fixes her fake smile and resumes in her high octave voice. "I know the way."

"I'll follow regardless," Pippa says. "I need to secure the perimeter."

Huh? "You're a security guard?"

"MCPD," Pippa says with a proud nod. "But yes, I am working security at the Mansion."

"Is it normal for police officers to be security guards?"

"With Mayor Bradford Walsh... yes."

The women stare at each other in silence. Pippa's eyes narrow, and her head slowly tilts.

"Why do I feel like I know you?" Pippa whispers.

Cara turns away, lifting her skirt to hurry to the balcony. A soft touch runs from her shoulder and down her arm. Cara stops, gazing over her shoulder at Pippa's hand.

"I'm going back inside to the party," Cara whispers.

"I do know you. Don't I?"

"You're mixing me up with one of the other hundred blonde girls inside with big poofy dresses."

Pippa locks onto her eyes. "Why are you here?"

"I was invited." Cara lays her bubbly voice on thick. "I come every year."

"Love, don't go looking for trouble."

Shit. She knows.

A flash of water, sheets, pillows, and heartbeats shutters through her mind.

Cara pulls her skirt high and runs back towards the rose garden. Pippa calls out to her, but she doesn't stop running until she clears the rear of the building.

Two men in dashing evening suits enter the rear opening of the Mansion.

Game time.

Cara shakes out her limbs and cools down her face. She walks as steady as she can in her baby blue heels and nears the entry.

A man in all black, an obvious cop, looks Cara up and down and then nods for her to enter.

Why is this so easy? Does the Mayor's son want to get caught?

Inside could be mistaken for a dingy club in the Nightclub District. The kind the Province kids don't hang out at. Yet, here they all are, sitting around roulette tables or mulling over cards at poker tables.

Inhaling her gasp, Cara bites her lip at the sight of piles of cash. Two men in all black standby, but Cara notices how they are easily distracted by the girls in bunny lingerie carrying drinks.

Come to Mumma, she thinks, eyes focused on the cash. *All my Christmases have come at once.*

She giggles to herself, never having opened a birthday or Christmas present in her life.

Her heart pounds with excitement. *What a payday.*

"Masks aren't needed down here," a ridiculously handsome man wearing a velvet evening jacket says. "You can relax and get a cosmo."

Cara taps her mask and smiles. "I love the added mystery the mask gives me. Especially in this setting."

"Yeah, it's pretty easy to upstage my dad's party."

"Oh, you're the Mayor's son?"

Caden smiles, intrigued. "You didn't know who I was?"

Cara grins. "Does that bother you to not be on someone's radar?"

"It's just a surprise." Caden pulls two champagne flutes from a nearby server's tray and hands one to Cara. "So, who are you, mystery girl?"

"Just enjoy the mystery."

"Why don't I know you? Who told you about tonight?"

"Why do you have to know? You can't know everyone here."

"It's my job as a Walsh to know everyone here."

"It's not my fault you're bad at your job."

Caden throw his head back as he laughs. "Who are you? You're so different to the other girls."

Cara smirks. "Good observation."

"Go upstairs," Caden whispers, nodding to the rear door.

"I thought I was here to party?"

"Oh, you are. My private party. Upstairs."

"In the ballroom?"

"No, my suite. Tell the guards your Caden's girl and they'll let you straight in."

"And what's in store for me up there?"

Caden traces her jaw and then drops his finger to her chest, running it along her cleavage. "The best night of your life."

Gross.

"You're coming with me?" she asks, trying to work out his game plan.

"I have to make nice with some people at the card tables," Caden says, dropping his hand by his side. "You go upstairs and make yourself comfortable. I'll be up in ten minutes and we will have a little fun."

Ten minutes alone in his bedroom to grab what I can. Then come back down here and take some cash while he's finding me upstairs. Sounds like a plan to me.

"Which way to your suite?"

Caden tells her which stairs and corridors to take. Cara hurries to the rear door, giving herself as much time as she can upstairs. Her eagerness most likely delighting Caden, thinking she can't wait to get into bed with him.

Cara walks a hall littered with pricey artwork, dressed with a plush rug, and lined with gold framed furniture. She turns left into the hall which will lead back to the ballroom. She closes in on a winding, oak staircase. Two guards stand at the top.

"Miss?" a cop in a pristine black suit calls. He walks up the hall, looking her up and down. "Can I help you?" He stops in front of her and looks at the hall behind her. "Where did you come from?"

Cara twists a lock of hair, using her club experience to good use. "Caden told me to stop by."

The officer snorts and rolls his eyes. "Another Caden girl. You can wait upstairs with the other two in the suite."

Cara's enthusiasm dwindles. "Other two?"

"I'm sure you're all very special," the cop says, masking his sarcasm terribly.

He smiles and gestures to the stairs.

Why is this so freaking easy?

With a shrug, she ascends the staircase. The guards at the top part ways. She moves between them with a sinking feeling that the easier this is, the more trouble it must be.

She moves into the suite and two girls walk towards the doorway, giggling at one another. Cara halts, worried they'll scream and rat her out to a guard as an imposter.

"Hey, did Caden send you up?" one girl asks Cara.

"Uh, yeah."

"Caden's down at the basement party," the other girl says. "We're heading down to get more face time with him."

"Oh, ok," Cara replies slowly.

"He told us to wait up here, but he's probably forgotten about us," the first girl adds. "I mean, a third girl? When he hasn't even started with us?"

Eww!

"Like I'm going to let him forget me," the other girl declares.

They leave, arms linked, and giggles galore.

Good lord...

Cara shakes her head, moving into the next room. *Gaga over a guy who clearly cares less about them. And they are teaming up to get him into bed?*

Sick!

Now alone, Cara looks around the bedroom, wishful a secret vault is left open with a buttload of gold pouring out. But then again, how would she carry it out?

Ok, Caden, what have you got for me?

She sorts through the bookcases, desk, shelves, and bedding. Small electronics, jewellery and drugs will all turn a profit on the streets. The Neons give her quick cash. The one thing they're good for.

She takes a gold Rolex, diamond encrusted cufflinks, a roll of hundred dollar notes, and enters the walk-in robe. She adds more goodies into her pockets and returns to the bedroom. One final scan of anything she may have missed, then it's on to the next room.

"You're all alone, mystery girl," Caden's voice sounds from the doorway.

Cara freezes.

Crap. He was quicker than I anticipated.

Over her shoulder, Caden leans against the doorframe. His tie unravelled and his jacket removed. He moves into the room and a thick brunette curl hangs over his forehead.

"Looking for something?" he asks, landing in front of her.

"Um. You?"

Caden smirks, folding his arms. "That so? I thought I left two girls up here?"

Cara shrugs. "I'm more than enough fun for you."

"I don't doubt it." He grabs her waist, thrusting her towards him. "Now, tell me who you are."

Cara pulls the tie from his neck and plays with it between her fingers. "Your dream girl."

Caden latches onto her wrist, his grip forceful. "Then you know my dreams are rough."

Cara's seductive smile disappears as a frown displays her displeasure.

So much for another dumb rich boy I can mess with. Who the hell is this guy?

Caden forces Cara to her knees.

Oh, no you don't!

Flashes of kneeling on church pews, on her knees to receive a beating, and slapped so hard she fell to her knees, rush through her mind. No one plays her like that anymore. No matter the money. No matter the status. This man will not overpower her.

She shoves him, and off guard, he stumbles backwards.

He leans forward and grabs a chunk of her hair. In a low whisper by her ear, "You like it rough, too?"

Cara yelps in pain. He cups her neck, and he yanks her backwards. She wrestles against his grip and trips over her dress, landing on the floor.

The gold Rolex spills out of her dress and skids against the carpet.

"You're stealing from me?" Caden says, astounded. "Well, well. You're certainly not boring."

An entertained smile curls his lips. Cara crawls against the floor, but he pulls her back. Her dress again betrays her.

He flips her over and lays against her body.

"Let me go!" she yells and spits at his face.

"*Ugh.*" Caden wipes his face and then backhands her face. "Gross, bitch."

Before Cara can react, Caden paws her dress, tearing at the bustline. The straps Gene made break easily.

Caden's ravenous hands creep into her dress. A surge of hatred fills her. Hatred for every vile person who has ever attacked her. For every time, someone thought they could use her. Every moment combines in her brain.

She bursts through the searing pain of memories. Her fist smacking into his face.

His head flies back, and she's quick with two more punches.

He falls backwards onto the floor and Cara scrambles to standing. She races to a small cupboard and reefs it away from the wall. While Caden writhes on the ground, Cara propels the cupboard forward. It tumbles over, landing on Caden's lower half.

Pulling her dress above her bust, Cara suppresses her sobs and flees the room.

Home

Pippa moves through the hall, patrolling her colleagues more than the Masquerade Ball guests. She took video in Caden's basement party and sent it to Captain McNeil. She still holds onto dear hope her Captain is an honourable cop. He took her under his wing, and he never attends events held by members of the upper-class.

Help me nail this guy, Cap. Please, be in my corner.

As she waits for her Captain's response, she paces the rose garden, but cannot keep away from the illicit acts happening in the basement. She moves to the rear of the building to take photos of other civilians entering the building.

A body bursts out of basement entrance, stuffing wads of cash into the mess of blue fabric as she races across the lawn.

"Cara?" blurts out of her mouth.

Cara's holds her dress high and her feet are bare.

"Hold up," Pippa says with hands in the air. "Let me help you."

"Get out of my way!" Cara wails, her masked face pale with fright.

She shoves Pippa out of the way with overpowering force. Pippa's foot twists, and she lands hard on the ground. In the time it takes to straighten herself out and check no security are on her tail,

Cara has already cleared the rose garden.

Getting herself up and forcing weight on her foot, Pippa stretches her neck, and then pursues Cara. Cara is racing towards the high brass gate, and Pippa is sure her stomping feet are going to crack the pavement below.

Beyond the gate, Cara is still running. Ahead of her is Abadi Mansion and Roth Manor. Two wealthy family estates who will not welcome a girl like her inside.

"Cara!" Pippa screams, her throat burning as she runs. "Cara, stop! Stop!"

She gains on Cara, hearing a lump bursting in her throat and a gasp breaking out.

"Cara!"

Cara's pace slows. Her breathing is loud and followed by sobs. She screams, stopping in place and tumbling forward in agony.

"Cara," Pippa says frantically, wrapping her arms around her. "It's ok. I've got you."

Cara collapses, an ugly cry gurgling out of her.

"What's happened? Was it Caden?"

"Let me go."

"I'm so sorry," Pippa whispers. "I should have warned you about him. I should have urged you to go home."

"He told me to go upstairs," she mumbles. "I thought I had time. But he... He..."

"He harassed you?"

Cara shivers. "I thought I had the perfect plan."

"What were you trying to achieve?"

Cara shoves Pippa off her. Screaming, Cara tears off her mask and rips the pins out of her hair.

"Come with me," Pippa says, steadily taking Cara's hands. "Come home with me. I'll take care of you."

Cara staggers in place, grim and tear-stained. "I'm so tired."

Pippa catches her limp body. "I've got you. I'll keep you safe."

Disrespect

Caden groans under the credenza. His gut cramping and his oxygen low.

"Sir," Jenkins calls, racing into the room.

He lifts the unit off Caden, and Caden coughs as it frees him.

"Sir, do you need me to call for medical attention?"

"No. Where did the girl go?" Caden asks, pulling himself to standing.

"Which girl?"

Caden spits blood from his mouth and wipes the sweat off his bruised face. "Blonde, blue dress, killer right hook."

"A girl was seen fleeing the room. The guards weren't aware there had been an altercation where you were in trouble. We assumed—"

"—What?" Caden bellows, his abdomen inflaming. "That typical *me* tried to force her into something and that's why she ran?"

"I didn't mean any disrespect, Sir."

"Just find her!" Caden yells, picking up his glass with a dreg of vodka but enough ice cubes to soothe his throbbing forehead. "I'm not done with her."

Jenkins clears his throat before continuing.

"What?" Caden sighs. "What is it? Spit it out."

"We saw Jackson follow the girl."

"*What*?" Caden yells. "I thought you were taking care of her? Find them both. Now!"

"On it. We'll secure the perimeter. They won't get out."

"You're already behind. Do better than that," Caden orders.

"Yes, Sir," Jenkins replies, running out of the room.

Caden collapses on the bed, his head throbbing.

Bitch.

Perfect

Jazz leans in and kisses her father's cheek in the foyer of Walsh Mansion. "Hope you had a pleasant night, Father."

"It was a swell evening," Darius says, smiling. "It's just getting late for me. The doctor suggests taking it easy, and I think I've done more than he recommends."

Jazz feels the familiar prick of tears that occurs with any mention of her father's ailing health. His heart condition hasn't improved in months, and the thought of losing him weighs on her heavily.

Darius holds out his hand to Adrian. "Good to see you again, Adrian."

Adrian shakes Darius' hand, trying to remain collected. "You too, Sir."

"I hope to see more of you," Darius says. "I've never seen my daughter this happy."

"I'll stay around as long as she'll have me," Adrian says, brushing his hand against Jazz's.

Tingles under Jazz's skin bump away any sadness, and her heart balloons.

"Mr Abadi," a valet attendant interrupts. "Your car has

arrived."

"Thank you," Darius says with a nod. He kisses Jazz's hand. "See you soon, my dear. Enjoy the rest of your evening."

"Take care, Father," Jazz says. The words *I love you* catch in her throat. Her heart begs her to say them, but her robotic upbringing keeps the words latched.

Her father smiles, seeming to know her internal pain. "I love you, Jazz."

Without further prompting, a tear streaks her cheek, and the words rush out of her. "I love you too."

He smiles and turns towards his car, a short wave of goodbye as he leaves.

Adrian wraps his arms around her, silent as his head rests by hers.

Jazz takes a long exhale and gestures for him to follow her towards the ballroom.

They sit at their table, and Jazz gazes at the bored faces, who look for gossip to stimulate their evening. Jazz finds herself missing the quaint dining room of the shelter.

Sachi swishes in the centre of the dancefloor, demonstrating dance moves which require confidence and a flair for fun. Jazz cups her mouth as she giggles at her young friend.

"Having fun?" Adrian asks, slipping a hand on her thigh.

Jazz smiles at him and says, "No."

Adrian's face falls. "Oh. Really?"

"I'm glad we came, but I don't feel like I belong anymore." Her smile remains. "I don't know if I ever truly belonged, but before it was all I knew. I enjoy being here for the connections. Connections will help us continue to fund the shelter. I can just do without the fanfare."

Adrian grins, slouching in his seat. "The food has been great. The band played great music. We look fantastic. And I'm so glad you're over it too."

"Want to get out of here?"

"Just say the word."

Jazz kisses his cheek and whispers, "Will you come home with me?"

"You mean...?"

Jazz nods. "Will you come home with me? To my bedroom. Stay the night?"

He swallows hard and nods slowly.

Jazz giggles. "Don't act too eager or anything."

He laughs nervously. "Believe me; I'm cheering inside my head. My outside is just trying to catch up."

Jazz clutches Adrian's hand, leading him into her home. The Abadi Mansion is stark quiet, allowing Jazz to hear Adrian's breathing behind her. She peers over her shoulder, and he is calm on the surface.

His smile is perfection.

If perfect exists, it's him.

"Ready to come upstairs with me?" she whispers.

"Yes," he whispers back.

She leads him to the dual winding staircases and takes him up the left-hand side to her suite.

"I can't believe you grew up here," Adrian whispers as he takes in her expansive bedroom.

The gauzy canopy of her four-poster bed sways with the wind, and her silk sheets are turned down, awaiting them.

Jazz runs her hands up Adrian's arms and lays a kiss on his lips. His hands run down the back of her dress, making her smile in the kiss.

She turns around and asks, "Will you unzip me?"

Adrian gulps and his hands tremble as they reach her zipper. After a cute struggle with the tiny, invisible zipper, he pulls it down, opening the back of Jazz's dress.

Jazz steps out of the dress, running her hands down the black and nude-coloured lingerie.

"*Wow*," Adrian says, breathlessly.

Jazz unravels Adrian's tie and slowly unbuttons his shirt. His hands creep around her hips, and she bites her lip. She's ready to spend the night with him, and hopes she doesn't sleep a wink. She opens his shirt and pulls it off his shoulders and down his arms. Her hands spread across his torso. Now knowing the origin of his scars, has given them a closeness she's never felt before. His trust in her. She will move heaven and earth to protect him.

When the two undress, Adrian scoops her into his arms. He carries her to the king bed and lays her down like a priceless item. He kisses her neck, and she moans as her thighs slide against his body and presses her hands into his back.

"Make love to me," she whispers.

Adrian kisses her collarbone and tells her, "I love you."

"I love you. Always and forever."

Untouchable

Cara's exhaustion riddles her body on the walk from the elevator to Pippa's apartment. She's grateful the sirens of Pippa's cop car allowed them to get from Sovereign Hill to Province in a matter of no time.

"You want to change?" Pippa asks softly, her hand on Cara's back as they walk into the living room. "I can give you some clothes. Do you want a shower?"

"He touched me," is all Cara can answer.

Pippa frowns as she presses her forehead against Cara's. "I'm so sorry. I should have gone into the Mansion with you. Or taken you home. Protocol be damned."

"He put his hands inside my dress." Cara's mind replays the encounter on a loop. "He touched me. He grabbed me like I was his plaything."

"He's a disgusting animal."

Cara shudders. "My entire childhood, I was treated like nothing. Something to abuse or throw away. How can it happen again now? I ran, so I'd never be in that situation again."

"Don't blame yourself. You're not at fault."

"I'm usually more careful. I always see everything coming."

Bile flows up her throat. *Except the last few weeks where nothing has gone my way.*

"From birth, Caden has taken what he wanted. He's untouchable. His mistakes get erased. Well, no more. I'm putting what I saw on record." Pippa traces Cara's jaw with her finger. "Will you make a statement?"

"To cops?" Cara says with disgust. "Hell no."

"I'll be there."

"I don't trust cops. They are government. Government wants to destroy people like me. They look at me, they see The Limits."

"You can trust me."

Cara's breath catches in her throat. Pippa's eyes are familiar and scary. Something about the crinkles beneath them, their large, oval shape, and their position against her nose. Dread fills the pit of her stomach, and she thrashes against Pippa's grip.

"You see him?" Pippa whispers sadly. "You see him in my eyes?"

"What? How... How?"

"He's my cousin."

Cara bashes her arms against Pippa, wriggling against her. "Let me go! A cop and a Walsh? Stay away from me. You're disgusting!"

"Cara, stop," Pippa whispers, holding onto her. "Listen to me. I'm not one of them. They aren't a true Walsh family. My grandfather would be ashamed if he could see them now. I'm here to make things right. To take them down."

Cara thrashes again. "Stop. I don't want to hear it."

"I want to be honest with you."

"He hurt me!" Cara yells. "He hurt me!"

Pippa crumples against her. A light sob hisses out of her. "I know. I'm so sorry. He will pay for laying a hand on you."

"I've let people think they can have me, but I've always maintained control." Cara scrunches her eyes closed and exhales. "But not with him. He stole my power. How could he do that?"

"He won't get away with it."

"Make me forget," Cara says in a rush, pulling at Pippa's tie. She undoes her top buttons, and repeats, "Make me forget."

Pippa's hands sit against Cara's waist, her elbows lock. "Wait, don't."

Cara's eyes well with tears as she pushes closer to Pippa. Her hands move to Pippa's belt. "Please. Make me forget."

"Ok," Pippa whispers.

Pippa tugs Cara's body against hers. Her hands run into her hair and their lips press together.

Cara moans as Pippa's tongue slides against hers. She squeezes Pippa's bum, and their kiss intensifies. Pippa's fingers work at unlatching the buttons on Cara's gown. Cara unzips Pippa's trousers and slides them down.

Pippa pulls her lips from Cara's, as she hurriedly undoes her tie and breaks open her shirt. She moves behind Cara to free the lowest buttons and sends the dress to the floor.

With the dress at her ankles, Cara turns and races her hands into Pippa's hair, finding her lips with a hungry kiss.

Pippa lifts Cara and carries her to the bed. Cara lays back and lets Pippa move on top of her. She watches Pippa move across her body. Her eyes don't close. She only wants to see Pippa.

Only Pippa.

"Love me," Cara whispers in a moment of weakness.

Pippa meets Cara's eyes with sincerity. "I will."

React

Cara lays in Pippa's arms, her head on Pippa's rising and falling chest. She focuses on nothing but the way Pippa strokes her hair.

The front door buzzer sounds through the apartment.

Pippa rises from the bed, slipping Cara off her. She cranes her neck towards the open bedroom door. "Who could that be in the middle of the night?"

Cara grasps Pippa's hand. "Ignore it."

Pippa smiles and lays down with Cara.

The buzzer sounds again, and Pippa can't ignore it. She leaves the bed, pulling on a t-shirt as she says, "I'll just check on it and ask them to leave." She walks around the bed, pulling on a pair of checker shorts, and leans over the bedroom window to the street below. "There's a patrol car down there."

Cara sits up, tugging on the sheet as her knees scamper to her chest.

"They are probably checking on me because I didn't sign out of my shift." Pippa moves to Cara and kisses the top of her head. "Don't worry. I'll let them know I'm home and they'll go back on patrol."

Cara nods, squeezing Pippa's hand. "Ok."

Pippa leaves the bedroom and Cara listens to her at the front door, answering the intercom. "Hello?"

"Jackson. Let us up," a voice responds.

"Look, I'm sorry I didn't close out my shift," Pippa says into the intercom. "I was chasing a lead, but it didn't go anywhere. I'll file a report at the station in the morning."

"Jackson, it's important. Let us up now."

Cara listens to the silence at the other end of the apartment.

Don't let them up. Don't let them up.

"I understand if you can't say anything out on the street due to protocol," Pippa says. She huffs and adds, "Just make it quick, ok? It's late."

Cara listens to a different buzzer sound, and her heart sinks. *Pippa is letting the pigs into the apartment.*

"It'll only take a minute," Pippa calls out. "It's probably a briefing about security at the Mansion."

Cara doesn't answer, instead taking the time of an elevator ride to plan her escape route. She takes clothes from Pippa's wardrobe to slip into. Her windows appear sealed shut, so escaping means dodging two or three cops in a well-lit, open-planned apartment. Cara is good, but she doubts she is that good.

Cara jumps as someone pounds on the front door. She throws on a tank top and shorts as Pippa opens the door.

"What's this about?" Pippa asks. There are murmured replies, and then she says, "Hey, what? What are you doing here?"

Pippa's anxious response gives Cara pause. Cara listens carefully to how many people have entered the apartment. They all move with heavy footsteps and it's hard to tell who is who.

"Heard you've been keeping tabs on me," a male voice says.

"Didn't make me too happy. I thought we were becoming friends."

"That's what you're here about?" Pippa asks with a shaky voice.

"Are you disappointed?" the male says with a throaty chuckle. "We can try to rekindle the friendship, if that's what you want."

"Jackson," another male voice says. "You need to stop the surveillance. We are putting you on notice. You were on our team to get with the program."

Cara does not like the sound of that and looks around the room for something to arm herself with. She rummages through the wardrobe, hoping to find something like a baseball bat.

"*Aw*, you got me a present," the first male voice says too close for comfort.

Cara looks to the bedroom doorway and Caden Walsh stands there, grinning maliciously. His image sends her into instant paralysation.

He wets his lips. "I missed you, mystery girl."

"Get away from her," Pippa yells. Cara hears a struggle in the other room, and Pippa yells again. "Let go of me! Get off me! Cara! Cara, are you ok?"

In a second, Caden grabs Cara and throws her down on the bed. He laughs, intensely staring into her eyes. Caden claws at her skin, her shirt riding up and her flesh inflaming. Caden pins her down, locking her arms under the weight of his knees. He pulls her shirt above her chest with glee.

An angry groan courses out of Cara as his hands tug at her shorts.

"Give in to me," he whispers, and the licks her neck.

"Cara!" Pippa screams in the other room.

Pippa's voice fills her with strength. She watches Caden have fun with her body and lets him sink into satisfaction. His bent legs lift off her arms and he slides down to reach more of her body. She waits. She doesn't react. He doesn't pay attention to her watchful eyes.

His chin juts upward, and *bam*. Her palm connects with his throat.

Caden splutters, choking to regain his breath.

Cara punches Caden's abdomen and wriggles against the bed to free her knee. She pulls her knee up and aims at his groin.

Caden stops her leg and pins her down. Sick frivolity dances in his eyes. He applies his body weight against Cara. Her face reddens and she gasps for air.

Cara summons her remaining strength and wraps her legs around Caden's torso. She squeezes as hard as her body will allow.

He yells in pain, and his hand swats, slapping a beating across her face. It sends Cara to release her legs, and in turn, he stops crushing her.

As Caden gasps heavily on top of her, she forces her fist into his gut. With a groan, he hits her back. Cara ignores the pain and wriggles against him to free herself, but Caden pins her shoulders back.

Caden stares into her eyes, and whispers, "I think we're made for each other."

"I'm no one's," she hushes.

Cara pushes against his weight and latches her hands around his throat. Before she can choke the life out of him, two cops in black suits race into the bedroom, guns drawn.

"Freeze!" they order, pointing their guns at Cara's head.

Cara's heart pounds. *I'm still the bad guy?*

So be it.

Cara punches Caden's nose. She forces him backwards and punches his face two more times. He falls off the bed and hits the carpet with a thud.

The guns cock, and Cara's heart stops.

This is it.

Two shots are fired.

Blinking rapidly, Cara takes in Pippa's gun, smoking after she shot each officer in the leg. The officers collapse to the floor and Pippa kicks away one gun and takes the other. She holds a gun over each dirty cops' head.

"You all right?" she asks Cara, keeping her eyes fixed on her colleagues.

Cara stares in shock. Blood oozing from the suits, and her attacker lies unconscious.

As Cara catches her breath, Pippa grabs a radio. "All units, two officers down at 137 Grange Street, Province, apartment 1606. One civilian unconscious. Another civilian, the victim of a sexualised attack."

Cara shoves Pippa. "Leave me out of it."

"He's not getting away with this."

Cara shoves her way out of the bedroom.

"Cara. Slow down," Pippa calls for her.

"Stop saying my name."

"Come back. I can't leave these guys out of my sight."

"Just stay away from me!"

Cara opens the front door and slams it behind her. She runs to the fire escape she used last time and descends like her life depends on it.

Arrangement

Pippa sits in the interview room, her knee bouncing with heightened energy. Her thoughts consumed with Cara. She wants to get this over with and find her as soon as possible. Protocol comes first. She needs the night's events on record so Deacon, Jenkins, and Caden Walsh will not get away with this.

This will be worth it. Staying here to get this on tape will be worth it. But I want to find her. Get her to safety. Make sure she's ok.

She spoke to Fitzpatrick, who met with her first. She kept her cool as she talked about her colleagues and the Mayor's son barging their way into her apartment. Like always, Fitz recommended dropping it. He didn't entertain her story long enough to hear about her fellow officers holding her back as Caden Walsh attempted rape.

She taps the steel bench with fury. When Fitzpatrick took no interest, she told him to leave and get Captain McNeil. She still believes McNeil isn't on the so-called payroll.

The interview room door opens. Pippa looks to the doorway with enthusiasm, only for it to immediately evaporate.

Mayor Bradford Walsh stands before her.

"Officer Jackson, I've heard a lot about you," Walsh says,

walking into the room and sitting next to Pippa.

"What are you doing here?" Pippa asks curtly.

"I'm here to see if we can come to some kind of arrangement."

"Arrangement?" Pippa scoffs.

"You shot two of my men and let my son be viciously attacked."

"Your men?" Pippa says with disgust. "The men who barged into my apartment in the early morning. The men who held me back as your son entered my bedroom and attempted to rape the woman inside."

Mayor Walsh's grin drips with venom. "My son did no such thing."

Pippa retches. "With all due respect, Sir, you were not there."

"Repeat after me. Caden was not in the apartment."

Pippa's eyes slit. "What?"

"Caden was not in the apartment."

"So, this is how you get people on your payroll?" Pippa says, staring down Mayor Walsh. "They speak the truth, get the real story out, and you swoop in and coerce them onto your side. You make them brush the story under the rug."

"You were in this precinct and keeping tabs on your colleagues," Mayor Walsh says, reclining on his seat. "And then we move you to Mansion security, and your wandering mind goes after my son."

"There's nothing wandering about it. Your son uses women for entertainment in broad daylight. In front of staff and the general public."

"No, he doesn't." The Mayor nods. "Try it. No, he doesn't."

"You will not put words in my mouth, Mr Mayor."

"You will redo your statement," Walsh says matter-of-factly. "You will recount a different version of events."

"How can you strive for such injustice?" Pippa asks in disbelief. "How can you not want your son accountable for his actions? To be held to a higher standard. To be worthy of the Walsh name."

Slap.

The Mayor's palm whacks Pippa's cheek, leaving behind a pulsating heat.

Pippa touches her cheek, her mouth falling open.

"You know it's an offence to assault an officer?"

Walsh chuckles. "Not for me." His expression drops as he leans in close. "And it doesn't have to be for you either. The bullet wounds to Deacon and Jenkins can be from an unknown assailant."

"I was protecting an innocent civilian," Pippa defends. "I wasn't in the wrong. It had to be done."

"You silly girl. You know better, about how we can spin that."

Pippa's jaw tightens and her hands ball into fists.

"You don't want your career in ruins before it begins, do you?"

"Why don't you end it? What possible reason could you have for keeping me around?"

"You've proven yourself quite the detective. Remarkable skills for a rookie. I could use someone like that on my team."

"And you think you can turn me?"

"You're a rule follower. You became part of my security team and never argued with the posting. Even when you knew it was a step down." Walsh tilts his head, a glint in his eye. "How about it? Want to take a step up?"

He must know I won't fall for it.

Walsh grins. "Clock's ticking."

"I want a promotion," Pippa blurts. "To detective."

"A mighty jump."

"Like you said, I earned it."

"So, you will stop keeping tabs on my son?"

"You'll see to the promotion?"

Walsh holds his hand out. "Yes."

Pippa shakes his hand. "Yes."

You have no idea who you are messing with, Uncle Bradford.

Pippa leaves the station, zipping her leather jacket and clenching her jaw against the chilly morning air. She pulls her hair loose from its messy bun and rolls her tight shoulders.

Is it still early enough for a bourbon?

With a tired huff, she moves to the sidewalk to hail a taxi.

"Hey," an emotionless voice calls from the right.

Pippa looks to the side where Cara leans against a building, clutching her arms across her body.

"Cara," Pippa whispers, moving towards her. "What are you doing here?"

Cara shivers against the wind, sliding down the brickwork. "You didn't want to see me again?"

"*Shit*," Pippa hisses, tearing off her jacket. She swings it around Cara's shoulders. "Here, quick, wear this."

Cara slips her arms inside the jacket, her teeth chattering.

"Of course I wanted to see you again," Pippa says, her emotions surging inside her. "I just didn't think you'd want to be around me again."

"Turned out I had no place better to go," Cara says with a

morbid smirk.

"Well, there's got to be someplace better than the police station. I don't want Walsh seeing you." Pippa pulls Cara into her arms, taking on her weight and moving her to the curb. "C'mon, let's get out of here."

"Can you take me to my brother?"

"You have a brother?"

"He's at this shelter."

"The one on Jordan Street?"

"Yeah. You know it?"

Pippa lets out a faint laugh of exhaustion. "I went there yesterday looking for you."

In the taxi's backseat, Cara cuddles against Pippa. Her breathing rapid and her body cold.

"What are you going to do about Caden?" Cara whispers.

"Make him wish he'd never been born. I pressured Walsh into giving me a promotion. I'll have greater access to tear this whole thing down from the inside."

"Why is this revenge thing so important to you? Why don't you walk away?"

Pippa holds her gaze. "It's my purpose."

Cara frowns and looks out the window at the buildings passing them by.

"You should get some sleep. Maybe a shower?" Pippa asks. "We could go back to my place first."

"No," Cara answers flatly. "Sorry, I don't want to go back to your place anytime soon."

Pippa nods. "I understand. I might have to move."

"You should keep it," Cara murmurs. "So I know where to find you."

"You will visit me again?"

"If I need you."

Pippa lifts Cara's hand and kisses it. "I don't want to lose you."

The car stops outside the Jordan Street shelter, and Cara slips her hand away and exits the car without another word.

Pippa pays the driver and exits the car, forcing her feet to follow Cara into the building.

Explain

Adrian's eyes lazily open. Soft sunlight filters into the bedroom, and he stretches out on the silky sheets and rolls onto his side. His lips curve into the happiest smile as his eyes gaze on the most spectacular woman he's ever known. Jazz smiles at him, her hair a gorgeous mess of raven curls and the ivory bedsheet tucked around her naked, olive-toned body.

"Good morning," she whispers in a sultry voice.

"Morning, Beautiful," Adrian replies, leaning in and kissing her softly. "Have you been awake long?"

"Just enough to watch you sleeping." She giggles. "You're cute when you sleep."

"Cute?"

"You look very peaceful." She kisses his nose. "It's a good thing."

He laughs. "Ok then."

Jazz's arm swings out and towards a small table. "You were so captivating I haven't looked at my phone yet."

"No," Adrian protests, flinging his arms around her and pulling her close. "Don't look at your phone."

Jazz giggles, collapsing against his bare chest. "It's the first thing I do in the morning."

"But I'm here now," he says, kissing the top of her head. "No phone."

Jazz drops her phone and presses her hands into his back. "How can I resist? Ok, you've got my attention."

He smiles. "Good."

"I could get used to my mornings being like this."

"Could we? I can't imagine not being at the shelter in the mornings. Or the evenings, for that matter. I dunno, like, it feels irresponsible."

Her fingers trace his jawline, and she stares into his eyes. "We're committed to each other, right?"

"Fully."

"We need to work on our relationship as much as we do the shelter. At some point, we need to decide if we will live together and where that will be. And I'm sorry, I'm not moving into the shelter."

"I never saw my life any other way since I moved in there."

"I can give you more."

"I don't know if I want more."

"We can hire people as caretakers. Look after the place and the people when we're not there."

"I dunno."

"I know it's scary, but the shelter is bigger now. It used to be a drop-in centre, but with my help, we can make it a much bigger community centre. We will need the staff, regardless. Why not use it to the advantage of our relationship too?"

He nods and kisses her cheek. "We'll work on it."

They unravel, and Jazz retrieves her phone. Adrian slides

down in the bed, smoothing his hair back as Jazz reads her phone screen.

"Pippa?" Jazz mutters.

"Huh?"

"Oh, Officer Jackson," Jazz answers herself. "It's a text message about Cara."

"What about her?" Adrian asks hesitantly. "You're talking with a cop about Cara?"

"I can explain."

"Explain what?"

She rubs her lips together and then says, "Cara came to me with a plan."

"Wait," Adrian says, disturbed. "Did you know she was going to the Ball?"

"Did you?"

He nods. "I saw her there. And now a cop is after her?"

"When Officer Jackson came to the shelter—"

"—There was a cop at the shelter?" Adrian yelps. "What? When? Why didn't you tell me?"

Her eyes droop. "Adrian, I..."

Adrian rubs his temples. "I think my head is about to explode."

"I'm sorry. I didn't mean for you to get hurt."

"I didn't stop her last night. By walking away, I let her rob those people." He exhales before asking, "How did you know she was there?"

Jazz sighs. "I got her the invitation and the dress."

Adrian's stomach sloshes like seasickness. "You didn't tell me?"

"I'm so sorry," she whimpers.

"It's ok," he soothes her, holding her closer. "Don't apologise. It's what Cara does. She talks people into circles until she gets into trouble."

"Don't be mad at her," Jazz whispers, wrapping her arms around him.

Adrian sinks into the bed. His fingers wander along the curve of Jazz's back as the bed sheet drapes around them.

"I love you," she whispers.

"I love you, too." Adrian kisses her softly. "We should get going."

"Yes. We need to see Cara," Jazz says. "Can we sit with my father before we leave?"

"He'll be ok about me having stayed the night?"

Jazz smiles, caressing his face. "He doesn't coddle me like that. He'll love to see you again."

"Sure. Let's go see him."

Stay

Cara crashes on a chair in the dining room.

"Are you ok?" Eddy asks, sitting by her. "You look like hell."

"Where did you go last night?" Aria asks, sitting across from her.

"Tessa didn't tell you?" Cara asks in a dry voice.

Gene places a glass of water in front of Cara. He pats her shoulder and gives her a strained smile.

Cara smiles at him. "Thank you."

"Tessa avoided me last night," Aria says, her lips twisting like she's working out a puzzle.

"She and Max were cagey," Eddy adds. "Did you get into some trouble?"

Eddy and Aria glance at Pippa.

"Don't interrogate her," Cara blurts, taking Pippa's hand.

"We weren't," Aria and Eddy say at once.

"I am a police officer," Pippa begins slowly. "But Cara's not in any trouble. She needs support."

"She has it here," Aria says, a sweet smile directed at Cara. "We'd love for you to stay, Cara."

"Where's Adrian?" Cara croaks, clearing her sore throat.

"He's not back yet," Gene says. "He stayed with Jazz last night."

"Oh," Cara replies, the word hanging there as she stares at Gene's young, fresh face.

"He'll be back soon," Eddy says. "You'll wait for him, yes?"

Cara nods. "Of course."

"Maybe you should lie down," Pippa suggests, rubbing a circle on Cara's back.

Cara rubs her head, nodding. "Feels like a killer hangover."

"You didn't sleep last night?" Gene asks.

Cara smirks, trying for humour instead of letting last night terrify her mind. "No time for that."

"C'mon," Pippa says, standing. "Let me take you to a bed."

"Oh, I wanted to let you know," Aria rushes to tell Cara. "I found my Rosary beads this morning. I'm sorry for doubting you."

Cara shakes her head. "Don't sweat it."

Cara walks out of the dining room, letting Pippa prop her up.

"Are you sure you don't want to make a statement or get an examination at the hospital?" Pippa whispers as they move through the hall.

"Don't."

"You know I'll make him pay."

"How do the Walshs not know who you are?"

"They haven't seen me since I was a kid, and I changed my name. I'll explain everything when you have rested."

"You came back!" Tessa exclaims, rushing down the hall. "Did you do it?"

Cara halts, disdain rising through her body at the sight of this girl. "Don't talk to me. I just went through hell. Try to follow Adrian's example and be a decent human being."

Tessa shrinks, her lips pouting and her eyes watering. "I, I... I'm sorry. I didn't mean—"

"—Get out of my way," Cara mumbles, pushing past her and forcing Pippa to hurry behind her.

"What was that about?" Pippa asks, following Cara into the bedroom.

"Nothing," Cara says, plonking down on a bed and burying her head into the pillow.

Cara wakes to a gentle stroke across her hair. Her eyes flutter open and she swivels her head. A blurry figure sits on the edge of her bed. She blinks a few times until she has a crystal clear image of Adrian.

"Morning," he whispers.

"Hey," she croaks. "How was your evening?"

"It was fine, but I want to know what happened to you?"

Cara frowns and pulls herself to sitting.

Adrian places his hand on her back, saying, "Careful, take it slow."

"I made a big mistake."

"I didn't want to follow you last night, because I was really mad at you."

"That's fair."

Adrian's hug is warm. "Tell me what happened."

Cara buries her face against his shoulder. "You don't want to know."

"Your face and arms are bruised. You look worse than after your last fight."

"I don't want to talk about it."

"I shouldn't have let you walk away from me. I figured you'd grab some jewels and get outta there before anyone could catch you. I never thought you'd get hurt."

"My plan was to stay invisible. It didn't work out as I expected."

"You've never faced the Mayor's security team before."

Cara uncovers her face and looks Adrian in the eyes. "It was his son. I thought I could outsmart him, but he plays by different rules."

Adrian holds her tight. "I'm so sorry. Jazz has told me about him in the past."

"I'm so stupid," Cara whimpers.

Adrian hushes her, rubbing her back soothingly. "No, you're not. It's ok."

Two sobs tumble out of her. "I love you so much. I'm so sorry."

"I love you too. You have nothing to be sorry about. I'm not mad anymore."

Cara pulls out of the hug, wiping her face dry. "Where's Pippa?"

"She's in the common room with Gene and Jazz," Adrian replies, hooking a finger under Cara's trembling chin. "Apparently Pippa met Gene's mum. How crazy is that? He's out there asking about his family. I think he's considering visiting them."

A limp smile tugs at Cara's lips. "It's scary to see your family again. But once you do, it's worth it."

Adrian smiles and whispers, "I'm glad I got to see you again."

"You say that like you know I'm leaving."

"I know you're leaving."

Mess

Caden stares at the pair of baby blue high heels. The mystery girl stumbled out of them during their tussle and Caden kept them as a trophy.

I will get you. I will make you mine.

"You had quite a night," his father announces, walking into his bedroom.

Caden rolls his eyes. "Why are you up here? You haven't come to my wing since I was ten-years-old."

"You look like hell," Bradford scowls. "Your face is hideously bruised."

"Just some rough playtime," Caden mutters. "You know how it is."

Bradford clears his throat. "I'm here to inform you I cleaned up yet another one of you messes."

Caden's interest piques. "Come again?"

"Your little event under the ballroom. Photos were leaked to Captain McNeil. You're lucky I was already at the police station, roping in another officer to our team."

Astounded, Caden stands. "That's it? I hold an event in the basement, with illegal gambling and strippers, and there's no fallout?"

"You disappointed me in many ways. I didn't see you dance with one suitable lady in the ballroom."

Caden's minds spins with confusion. "Your concern is about my lack of a date? Are you mad?"

"The lovely Rory Briar was asking about you," Bradford says, looking over the artefacts askew on the dented credenza. "I've done business with her father. It would be very beneficial to have a closer relationship with the Briar family."

"Dad, can you get out of here? My hangover is about to bore through my skull."

"Since you failed to find the right woman, I've done it for you," Bradford states. "Rory Briar. Make it happen."

His father leaves the room. Exhausted, Caden flops back on his chair and scrolls through his phone. He lands on the contact information for Rory Briar.

A boring girl? That's who he sees me with? We will see about that.

He clicks *call* and lifts the phone to his ear.

Can I turn a good girl bad?

"Hello, Rory here."

"Rory, sweetheart, how are you doing?"

Rory is all giggles on the other end. "Um, hi. Yeah, I'm good. This is Caden, right?"

"Caden Walsh," Caden replies, needing to hear his full name.

"I saw the name on my phone, and hoped I wasn't hallucinating," she says bashfully. "I'm so glad you called. I wanted to see more of you at the Masquerade Ball, but you seemed to go missing."

"Don't fret, I could never forget that pink dress."

Rory giggles girlishly.

"I'd be honoured to take you out sometime. Are you free this weekend?"

"Oh my gosh," Rory cheers. "This is so exciting. I can't this weekend. We have a family reunion at my father's cabin. But could we meet up the following weekend?"

Caden's eyebrows raise and he bites his lip. Her rejection of this weekend leaves him curious.

I can work with a girl who says no.

"Sure. That'd be great." His voice smooth and swarve. "I'll call you next week to set up our date."

"Oh, yay. I can't wait!"

"I promise you, you've never had a date like I can deliver."

"I believe that, Mr Charming."

"Take care, Rory. Talk soon, beautiful."

Caden laughs as Rory almost explodes from the word *beautiful*. He ends the call and tosses his phone, bored again with his life. He had a stimulating girl who fought against him, and she slipped through his fingers.

Sometimes I wish I didn't get away with things.

I wonder what jail feels like.

Could I ever actually get there?

He grunts out of his chair and throws himself onto the bed.

"Clements! Clements!" Caden yells, stretching out on his giant bed.

"Sir?" Clements asks, entering the room.

"Get the largest bottle of vodka from the freezer and bring it up here."

"As you wish, Sir," Clements says, and leaves the room.

Caden groans, his head throbbing from the two beatings he took last night.

How many risks do I have to take?

When will it be enough?

He looks at Rory's profile picture on his phone.

Only one way to find out.

Luck

Cara steps into the common room and sits on the couch by Gene. "Hey."

"Hey. So, last night didn't go as planned?" he asks.

"There was one person who didn't play ball like I expected."

"I'm glad you're ok."

"I listened to you and didn't get myself killed."

"Did your cop friend help with that?"

Cara breathes out gradually. "Yeah. She really did. You talked to her about your parents?"

"She went to a domestic dispute at their house," Gene tells. "I don't think I want to go back there, but I want to let my mum know I'm ok. Pippa says she could arrange a mediated meeting."

"I hope it goes well for you."

Gene nods. "If I go through with it."

"Good luck with your decision. Now, I don't want to see you in the Nightclub District," Cara says, tussling Gene's hair.

Gene groans, pulling his head away from Cara's reach. "You won't."

"Seriously. I've got enough stuff to worry about. Don't make looking out for you another thing added to my list."

"Stop nagging me," Gene grumbles. "Fine, I won't go. You happy?"

Cara laughs. "Peachy."

"They're all too old for me, anyway. I got what I was looking for and turned out it wasn't for me." Gene crosses his arms and stares at the floor. "I can't believe I'm gonna miss you."

"I'll miss you too, Gus."

Gene *tsks* and rolls his eyes.

"I'm just kidding," Cara teases. "I'm giving you ammunition to not miss me."

"Thanks, psycho," Gene says, grinning.

"I'll see ya round," Cara says, getting off the couch and giving him a wave.

"Hey," Pippa says, as Cara walks over to her and Jazz.

"Hey," Cara says, awkwardly folding her arms.

"I have something for you," Jazz says. She holds out a small black phone with large buttons.

"A burner phone?" Cara questions.

"Just for emergencies," Jazz explains. "Or, if you want to get in contact. I know it would mean a lot to Adrian to speak to you more often."

Cara allows Jazz to place the phone in her hand. "I dunno."

"I put my phone number in there, Adrian's office line, Eddy's—
"

"—No," Cara blurts. "No, I don't want their numbers."

"I thought you'd want to speak to them more than me," Jazz admits. "You could add Pippa's number too."

Pippa immediately reaches for the phone.

Cara tugs it away. "No. Sorry." She gently touches Pippa's

cheek. "I can't have us in such easy contact."

Pippa drops her hand, not saying a word.

Cara gives the phone to Jazz. "Only your number. I can't have Adrian's. If Adrian or Pippa need to talk to me, they have to come to you, and you have to make the call."

"Why?" Jazz asks, perplexed.

"You and I have no love lost. You won't call me unless someone is dying. I need that barrier. I need that space."

Jazz goes through the contacts and deletes entries. "If you're sure?"

"I'm sure." She looks to Pippa and smiles. "Do you understand?"

"No, but yes," Pippa says with a smile.

As Jazz hands the phone back, Cara asks, "Does Adrian have the number?"

Jazz shakes her head. "No. I hadn't told him about the phone yet. I wanted to gauge your reaction before telling him."

Cara smirks. "My, my. You are smart. I'm so glad my brother is with someone so perceptive."

"Not my first day here," Jazz says with thinly veiled sarcasm. "Also, remember your name is on the deed to this building. I hope loyalty will bring you back more often."

Cara shrugs. "Thanks for the phone."

"Take care of yourself," Jazz says.

"Did you speak to the Mayor?" Cara asks.

Jazz frowns. "No, I didn't get a chance. My father was unwell, and I didn't want to upset him."

"Do you think you'll have another chance?"

Jazz nods. "Absolutely. Adrian and I sat down with Father this morning. We explained out concerns about The Limits and he suggested holding a dinner party. At my home, I can speak to Mayor Walsh one on one."

"Are you sure that's a good idea?" Pippa asks hesitantly. "Do you want to get mixed up in this?"

"I've done business with the Walsh family in the past," Jazz says. "I was blind to the seedy underbelly of Bradford Walsh's dealings. But I'm not anymore, and I need to step in."

"You and I need to talk before you meet with him," Pippa tells Jazz. "I have information that will be useful to you."

"Certainly. Glad to hear it."

"And I'm available to help you all whenever you need it," Pippa says. "If anyone comes in here, running from abuse or other danger, I will help however needed. I know it's not commonplace around here to get help from a cop, but I am truly on your side."

"I'd be grateful for that," Jazz says, hand over heart. "You'll have to sit down with Adrian and Eddy and gain their trust."

Cara steps away from the two women. "I'm going to say goodbye to Adrian before I leave."

She moves into the hall and finds Adrian speaking with Max. She waits in the hall, arms folded, wondering if Max is confessing to his part in last night's events.

Adrian pats Max's shoulder and the two part ways.

"Have you decided to stay?" Adrian jokes, walking towards her.

"You seem so happy here," Cara says, unable to quit her grin.

"I am happy."

"You're just such a natural at talking to people. I guess that's why I slowed down for you."

"I'll slow you down anytime you need it."

Cara embraces her brother and sighs. "I promise to come back. I'm sorry I left you hurt for so long."

"Remember to stop punishing yourself. You don't have to be alone. Plus, looks like a good woman is head over heels about you."

Cara laughs as the two break apart. "She is foxy, isn't she?"

"Are you going to stay with her?"

Cara shakes her head. "No, I'm staying on my own. A lot has happened over the last few days. Quiet and darkness helps me process."

"Be safe out there."

"I will. You stay safe here." Cara chuckles, and adds, "I doubt that kickass woman will let anything bad happen to you."

They hug again, and Cara knows it's time to leave.

Pippa walks Cara out of the shelter, gripping her hand firmly.

"Your dress is at my place," Pippa says. "The officers who attended my apartment, after I radioed in, wanted to bag it for evidence. I told them Caden left evidence on it, so they left it behind and took me to the station instead. Everything you had stowed away is there."

"That's the first lucky break I've had in over a month."

"You wanna come with me and grab it?"

"Ditch the dress and keep the rest. I gotta settle a few things, and then I'll take them."

"Don't go out on your own," Pippa pleads. "You've just gone through some horrific trauma. The worst thing for you is solitude. Stay here. Stay with your family."

Cara kisses Pippa like it's her last day on Earth. "My whole life is trauma. Being on my own is the only way I've found peace."

"But you steal money and barely eat."

"It's my life. Let me live it."

Pippa's eyes well, and she pulls Cara into a hug. "You break my heart."

"Can you check in here? Make sure Adrian is doing ok?"

"Of course. But what about when he asks about you? Will I be able to let him know you're ok?"

"Just tell him I'm ok. Because I will be."

Pippa pulls out of the hug, holding onto Cara's forearms and staring into her eyes. "I'm not losing you."

"Just let me be. I need to process everything." Cara leans in and kisses Pippa softly. "I'll be back for you. It's just... so much of my childhood has come back to me. I need time alone."

"I trust you to look after yourself. Just don't forget me."

Cara smiles. "Impossible."

Run

Jazz wraps her arms around Adrian's shoulders. They sit on his bed after a whirlwind of a day.

"How are you doing?" she asks.

"I'm ok." He kisses her cheek. "How could I not be when I have you? But all the Cara stuff... Ah, man."

"I know. It's a lot."

"I wish she didn't need to run."

Jazz nods. "She's been through so much, I could never understand."

"I wish everything we went through together was enough to keep her around."

"You need faith she'll come back."

"Yeah, I guess."

Jazz's phone rings in her pocket. She unravels her arms from around him, and asks, "Do you mind?"

"Go ahead."

Jazz retrieves her phone and looks at the caller id. *Sachi Yuki.*

Surprised, she answers the call. "Hello? Sachi?"

"Jazz," Sachi says in a panic. "Jazz, I'm going to lose it."

Jazz stands in alert. "Sachi, what's wrong?"

Sachi's ramblings are fast and jumbled. Her anxiety heightens her pitch.

"Sachi, slow down. Tell me what's wrong."

The line goes dead.

"Sachi?" Jazz shrieks. "Sachi? Hello?"

Adrian stands in front of her, his alarm matching hers. "What's going on?"

"It's my friend Sachi. You met her at the Masquerade Ball. She was wearing a black and white dress." Jazz's stomach somersaults. "I need to call her back. Something terribly wrong has happened."

To be continued…

THANK YOU FOR READING

To continue with the **Happily After When** Series, look out for the following books:

      #1 – JAZZ

      #2 – ARIA

      #4 – SACHI

      And many more to come!

Other books by Emily Bourne are the **In It Together** Series:

      #1 – In A Mirror

      #2 – In The Haze

      #3 – In It Together

      #4 – In The Beats

      And many more to come!

CONNECT WITH THE AUTHOR

Visit author **Emily Bourne** in the following places:

Website: www.emilybourne.net
Instagram: @iemilybourne
Twitter: @iemilybourne
Facebook Page: Emily Bourne: Author
YouTube: Emily Bourne

www.ingramcontent.com/pod-product-compliance
Lightning Source LLC
Chambersburg PA
CBHW050809190726
48285CB00005B/1855